SKINNERS

Adam Millard

Bizarro Pulp Press
www.BIZARROPULPPRESS.com
Skinners Copyright © 2013 Adam Millard

ISBN-13: 978-0615755762
ISBN-10: 0615755763

All rights reserved. No part of this book may be
reproduced or transmitted in any form or by any means,
electronic or mechanical, including photocopying,
recording, or by any information storage and retrieval
systems, without the written consent of the publisher,
except where permitted by law.

Printed in the USA.

The car screeched along the slick tarmac. Its bullet-riddled body gave it the appearance of a cheese-grater on wheels. The man behind the wheel was Russian, not that it was immediately apparent; he wasn't wearing a ushanka or whistling a Soviet ditty.

He floored the car, taking it up to almost eighty. It didn't matter, though, as the street was deserted, apart from the man stepping out into the road. The man aimed his gun towards the approaching Audi.

The driver, realizing he was about to be fired upon, dragged the wheel hard to the right. The car whined as the rubber left its tires, and then the tires left the road. The Audi began to somersault, one, two, three; the man with the gun gave up counting after that. He stepped aside and watched the wreckage drift by.

The car slammed into a storefront and came to a sudden stop, and only then did the man lower his weapon. Once again everything was silent.

"And cut!"

The man with the gun turned in the street as lights powered down, and people began to swamp the wreckage in the hope of finding Ivan unharmed.

"Can somebody get me a coffee?" Tom Harker, the weapon-touting actor, said. "I'm as dry as a fuck with no foreplay."

Somebody ran off set to fetch Mr Harker a latte with two sugars and no milk. *Definitely* no milk. The last person to bring him white coffee had been fired on the spot, and Tom had vowed never to work with them again.

"That was good," Michael Starkweather said as Tom sidled up alongside him at the edge of the road. Starkweather was the director of the first three Lethal Agent movies, and had decided to helm this installment on the proviso that Tom dropped his attitude. He hadn't. In fact, he was a bigger asshole than ever before, but it was too late now. Contracts had been signed, people had been paid, cameras had been switched on…

"Good?" Tom said, glancing around in anticipation of his coffee. "That was fucking *epic*. I don't like to blow my own trumpet, but that's got to make the final cut."

Starkweather watched the scene once again on the miniature screen. Shaking his head, he said, "I'm pretty sure Ivan was smiling as the car came towards you."

Someone handed Tom a steaming Styrofoam cup, which he checked before returning to the screen. Sighing with relief, the runner did some running, mainly in the opposite direction to Tom Harker, who was about to blow what little calm he possessed.

"Smiling? What the fuck would he be smiling at?"

"Look," Starkweather said, flicking the screen with his nicotine-stained finger. "That look like a grin to you?"

It did. That Russian sonofabitch was smiling in the take. Tom couldn't believe what he was seeing. "Where did you get him from?"

"Russia," Starkweather replied. "It's not like they have a store where you can pick up foreigners."

"He's got to go," Tom said, sipping cautiously at his coffee. He knew, as well as the rest of the crew, that the contents of a Styrofoam cup were deceiving. You could fill one to the brim with liquid magma and you wouldn't know until your innards were outards.

"I can't get rid of him, Tom," Starkweather said. "He's the main villain in this picture. If he goes, we're gonna have to shoot the last three weeks again."

"CGI," Tom said. "Just put a new face over his face."

Starkweather held out his hands. "What do you see when you look at me, Tom? Spielberg? Peter-fucking-*Jackson*? You think I have the money to stick a new head on the Russian in post-production?"

Tom burnt his mouth on the coffee and looked around for someone to take his anger out on. The crew was busy prepping the scene for a retake. Ivan, the grinning Russian sonofabitch, was being peeled out of the Audi. He offered Tom a thumbs-up; Tom gave him the middle finger.

"Don't be like that," Starkweather said. "I'll have a word with him, make sure he gets it right in this next one."

Tom lit a cigarette and exhaled a plume of blue-grey smoke into the director's face. "If he fucks it up on this one, Mike, I'm out of here."

"He won't. Just leave it with me. I'll—"

That was as far as he got before the ground began to shake violently. Most of the crew were knocked from their feet, and those left standing staggered comically from left to right like the crew of the Starship Enterprise whenever the ship was blasted by a Klingon Bird of Prey. Tom's Styrofoam cup seemed to move in slow-motion as it lurched from his grasp and came down on his groin, its scalding-hot contents all but cancelling his midnight rendezvous with B-movie starlet, Angelina Frost.

For almost a full minute, the earth rumbled and shook, preventing Tom Harker from tending to his steaming tackle, and when it stopped – *finally* – Tom knew that somebody, he didn't give a shit who, was going to get fired for this.

*   *   *

The vagrant barely woke from his drunken stupor as chunks of building landed all around him. It was only when a bottle smashed a few feet from where he lay that he muttered himself back into existence.

Pushing himself into a tidier pile – if that was, indeed, possible – he glanced around at the fallen debris.

"Picked the wrong fucking alley," he whistled through popcorn teeth. Then he saw the crack running the length of the alleyway. If he had fallen asleep a few feet to the left, he'd have fallen down it, probably still non-the-wiser as he sank to whatever depth it ran. "I'll be damned," he said, pushing aside the rags and newspapers that were his own special version of Egyptian sheets. He clambered to his unsteady feet and swayed as he tried to focus on the huge crack in the ground. He could see three of them, but if he closed his left eye…

Suddenly, something crawled out from the aperture. The vagrant almost toppled backwards, and would have had it not been for the large industrial bin to his left.

He watched as the strange, white thing scuttled

forward. At first, he thought it was a mouse. It was too big to be a cockroach, and too small for a rat.

But it was the purest white, speckled here and there with vivid colour. Bewildered, the vagrant stepped towards it, his one eye closed so that two of the trio were invisible. The creature must have sensed him approaching; it stopped crawling, and seemed to stare warily up at the bearded hobo.

It was a *beetle*. The vagrant was pretty sure of it now that he was close enough. He could see its shell and the six, wiry legs beneath it. Its shell was patterned, giving it the appearance of a clown's face. There was even a bright red nose in the centre of its back. Unless they had been performing illegal tests in the immediate vicinity – which wouldn't have surprised him – this was no mouse.

"You're a funny little fella, aintcha?" the vagrant said, reaching down with one filthy hand, a hand that was almost big enough to punch the Hulk out. "What's say I pick you up, huh?"

The beetle chirruped and shrank ever-so-slightly as the huge-knuckled vagabond hand enveloped it.

"There we go. Ain't never seen one like you before, that's for sure." He turned his fist over and opened it. It was then that he saw the teeth. Rows and rows of needle-sharp pins. The underside of the beetle looked like something you might use to extract information from an unwilling hostage. The teeth began to grind left and right, as if motorized, and the beetle chirruped once before flipping itself over onto the massive palm.

Then came the pain.

The vagrant screamed and tried to shake the creature off, but its teeth were in deep. "Motherfu—" he said before trailing off, as the agony tore through his entire body. He grabbed the beetle with his other hand and snatched it away. His palm – all of it – came away, revealing a perfect skeletal hand. He launched the beetle as far as he could down the dark alley, and was almost certain it made an excited *Wheeeeee!* as it went.

The hobo fell to his knees, trying to stem the flow of blood from his wide-open palm. It was impossible, and the pain was like nothing he'd ever felt before, even though he'd once been an altar boy.

The night was suddenly filled with chirrups. The vagrant looked up from his bloodsoaked hands in time to see more beetles, perhaps thousands, crawl their way from the crack in the ground. He fell back; his head connected with a gargoyle that had only a few minutes ago been perched atop the building beside the alley.

A second later he was covered with them. Hundreds of scurrying, chirruping, clown-faced beetles from the very depths of hell.

Ten seconds later they were gone, leaving behind a stripped carcass in a filthy overcoat. Even his tobacco-tainted beard had been devoured, which would give at least twenty of the creatures one hell of a fur-ball come sun-up.

*   *   *

The "A" Platoon of the LAFD were busy dousing the flames of an arson attack when the earthquake hit. Kyle Knowles had had a feeling that morning something serious was going to happen; he was like a cat, sensing the disasters before they happened. That morning, though, he'd convinced himself it was a false-alarm; what he was feeling might have been resultant of his insomnia or lack of nutrition. Now, with the earth trembling all around and the fire dancing in front of them like the Human Torch having an epileptic seizure, he knew he shouldn't have ignored his instincts.

With the cessation of the earthquake came a radio-call from base. Kyle made his way over to the truck and answered it. "We felt it," he said. "Had to be a six-pointer."

The voice that came back startled Kyle. He'd been expecting the calm, controlled voice of somebody unperturbed. What he got was a panicked, staccato whine of some dispatch virgin.

"We need you over on Highland Avenue ASAP," she screeched. Kyle moved his head an inch away from the radio. *"Some bad shit's going down over there, we don't know what."*

Kyle shook his head, depressed the button, and said, "What kind of bad shit? We've got a real run, here. Gonna be one hell of an overhaul come morning."

"Forget the fucking fire!" the dispatcher practically howled. *"Get everyone over to...wait a minute, the division chief wants to speak with you."*

Kyle counted to three in his head; all around him, the world continued to fall apart.

"Kyle, is that you?"

"Dan, it's me," he said. "You want to tell me what's going on over on Highland?"

There was a pause, the kind of split-second silence that had the ability to open bowels.

"The quake wasn't the worst of it," the chief said. *"There's police over there right now trying to calm things down, but...I don't know what they fucking are, Kyle. They're everywhere."*

"What?" Kyle said. "*What's* everywhere?" He stared off into the blazing inferno as the chief's voice told him something he could have done without.

"Clown-beetles," he said. *"And they're eating everybody in their path."*

Kyle dropped the radio and slumped against the side of the truck. It all made sense, now. That strange, ominous feeling he got whenever the shit was about to hit the fan. This was it. It all came down to a swarm of flesh-eating bugs.

He called his crew in, who were a little concerned that they were leaving behind a real conflagration to go off on a bug-hunt.

"Just trust me," he told them as they headed toward Hollywood Boulevard. "I don't think these are your garden-variety bugs."

*   *   *

Tom Harker lifted the gun and aimed it towards the swarmed figure. The tea-boy, poor little fucker, was covered with beetles. His screams were just about audible over the incessant chirruping of the bugs.

"What are you gonna do with *that*?" Starkweather asked as he hoisted himself up onto the overturned Audi, where Tom was taking aim at the beetle-enveloped kid. "It's a fucking fake, Tom. You think I'd ever give you a real gun?"

"Shit, Mike!" Tom spat. "We're fucked!"

The set was in chaos. People were running left and right in an attempt to escape the ferocious clown-beetles. Tom had seen three people completely skinned where they stood. One of them, Penny Jackson, he'd had high hopes of laying. He wasn't sure what pissed him off the most, the fact that he would never get the chance to taste her, or the fact that a hundred bugs had got there first.

"What the hell *are* those things?" Tom yelled. For some reason he continued to point the gun as if it was useful; he would have done more damage throwing it at the bug-engulfed runner.

"Beetles," Starkweather said, "though they're bigger than any beetle I ever saw, and they got teeth that'll bite your dick off quicker than you can pull your zipper up. No, they're something new, Tom. Or something *old*, even."

Tom, confused, scratched his head with the replica gun. "What, like dinosaurs?"

"I don't fucking know. Shit, Tom, for all I know they're ladybirds on a leery night out."

Just then, the runner's scream pierced the night. The bugs dispersed, leaving behind a bloody figure. Amongst the gore, a few beetles continued to feed. Either that or they were tangled up in the runner's intestines.

"Is he dead?" Tom asked.

The runner slumped to the ground with a slap, like meat on a butcher's counter.

"He is now," Starkweather confirmed.

The swarm rushed across the street in search of

somebody else to defile and devour. Around ten crew-members had locked themselves in Tom's trailer, which pissed him off more than the hungry creatures scuttling across his film-set. He was outside, among the carnage, while grips and fucking foley-artists were living it up in the safety of his trailer. Even the unprofessional Russian was in there. How wrong was that?

The beetles must have heard a sound from within the trailer, for they changed direction and disappeared beneath it.

"Do you think they can get in?" Starkweather asked.

"I fucking *hope* so," Tom muttered. The director shot him a reproachful glance. "Well, we're out here standing on an Audi's ass in the pissing rain. Better be *something* entertaining to watch."

At first nothing happened. People ran maniacally across the set, flicking away bugs that were desperately trying to peel the flesh from them, but neither Tom nor Mike were interested in those poor bastards, not anymore.

All eyes were on the trailer.

"Ten bucks says they get in," Tom said, offering his trembling hand to the director, who stared down at it as if it was coated in shit.

"What the hell," Mike said, shaking it. "Ten bucks says that trailer's more airtight than a spaceman's helmet."

From somewhere on the set came a scream. Mike could have sworn it belonged to Katie Myles, Tom's make-up artist, and for that reason he decided not to broach the subject with Tom. He'd go ballistic if he knew the woman that made him look pretty day in, day out, had just been chewed up and spat out like gristly beef.

"Hey, look," Tom said, jabbing a finger towards the trailer. "Something's happening."

He was right. The trailer was rocking back and forth, and not in the nice, let-off-some-steam sorta way at the end of a hard day's shooting.

"Doesn't mean anything," Starkweather said, although he knew he was mistaken. "They might just be climbing, to get to someplace higher up—"

"They're getting skinned," Tom said. He realised that he was smiling, which was slightly odd, even by his own sociopathic standards. "Look."

A body, or something like it, appeared at the window. Starkweather was reminded of something he had seen as a child; a red mannequin, standing naked and alone in the middle of a store. Why would they use red mannequins? How could you even tell if an item of clothing was going to look good on you if your basis of comparison was a red fucking mannequin?

Even though the red body was skinless, Tom

knew they were staring at Ivan. He'd recognise those teeth anywhere. The Russian was slapping at the trailer window; each time his hand connected with the glass a crimson geyser shot out from his open palm. Tom, for some superfluous reason, wondered how long it would take him to clean the trailer down when all of this was over.

Providing he survived in the meantime, of course.

The doors to the trailer flew open so hard they ricocheted back at the materializing mess. The emerging crew were dead; they just didn't know it yet. The swarm of clown-faced beetles skittered out through the open door, bloated and distended from their generous meal. Three or four – it was hard to tell *what* was coming through the door, such was the viscera and ichor – of the crew practically fell out onto the rain-drenched street, completely ignoring the three steps down from the trailer. Newcomer beetles swarmed over them but quickly realised they were already *sans* skin.

On top of the battered Audi, Starkweather handed Tom Carter fifty bucks from his wallet. Not that he would have the chance to spend it, unless somebody came to sort this mess out.

"We need to find somewhere safe," Tom said. "It's only a matter of time before they realise they've neglected us."

The director shoved the empty wallet back into his jacket pocket and sighed. "I'm all ears, O wise one."

Tom knew just the place.

*　　*　　*

The blonde reporter trembled nervously in front of the camera. All around, people were being flayed. She glanced cagily over her shoulder as a screaming lady ran past, coated with the little fuckers. This reporter, though, was too stupid to realize the danger she was in, and urged the cameraman to continue rolling.

"You're on, Gail!" the terrified cameraman yelled. He had to yell; people were screeching and gargling as they were torn apart. It was terribly inconvenient.

"We join you now from downtown LA, where something dreadful is unfolding. A swarm of creatures that can only be described as beetles, with a clown-like pattern on their shells, has begun to attack people in the street. I don't know whether you can see the sheer horror taking place behind me…" She broke off to point at random people being stripped bare by the bloodthirsty bugs. It would, she hoped, be enough to win her an award. Turning back to the camera, she said, "Just terrible.

Absolutely horrible. The way that old lady's face came off…just…not nice. Anyway, we can now confirm that the appearance of these beasts has been linked to an earthquake that occurred a little over an hour ago. I'm putting my…" She stopped talking as the cameraman began to frantically wave and point. "What? Paul, what are…" She felt something scuttle along her shoulder; a terrible rattle suddenly filled her earhole.

"Oh shit," she said as the creature crawled along her neck. A moment later, the bugs were all over her, peeling her like an overripe banana. The cameraman kept rolling until he, too, was devoured by the insatiable swarm.

Oh well, at least the news was out. These creatures and the terrible things they were capable of had gone live into the homes of millions of people.

At least they would have seen it if the cameraman had pushed the red button that recorded things in the first place.

*   *   *

The damage inside the Hollywood Wax Museum was minimal. Hugh Jackman had toppled over and was currently dry-humping Scarlett Johansson. In the next room Mahatma Gandhi had landed face down on Bill Clinton, a position that the former president was more than familiar with. The quake had toppled models over each floor; the only casualty was Kristen Stewart, who had fallen out of a third-floor window and now lay in several pieces on the street below.

"This is not good," Lisa said, surveying the damage. The waxwork likenesses stared up at her as if pleading for help.

"Could be worse," Angelina said, stroking the intact figure of Johnny Depp. "I don't know what I would do if I lost Johnny." She smiled, kissed the model on the cheek and slapped it, somewhat unceremoniously, on the ass.

A man charged towards them. His red, bloated cheeks suggested he had an agenda. A woman sporting a decent-sized purple bruise nervously followed him. "Excuse me, ladies, but I don't suppose we will be getting a refund for this, will we?" He gestured to the woman he was with, as if the ever-increasing swelling on her head would influence their decision.

"I'm sorry, sir," Lisa said, "but that will be up to the owners. I'd be glad to assist you and your wife to the front of house." To the woman, who seemed to be growing more ashamed as the seconds passed, she said, "Do you need a bandage for that?"

"Listen, *missy*," said the man, "I expect a full

refund. We didn't get to see half the exhibits, and I only fucking came for the horror display."

"Like she said," Angelina added from the side, "that'll be down to the proprietors, so you can stop taking it out on us. We only work here."

The man grabbed his wife by the hand and said, "Come on, Pleasance, we're going."

As he rushed away, with Pleasance in tow, the girls erupted with laughter.

"Fucking *Pleasance*," Angelina snorted. "I think my grandmother had a terrier called that."

"Can you believe that guy?"

"I'm pretty sure that wasn't his wife."

"What makes you say that?"

"Did you see a ring?" Angelina sniggered. "I'd say Pleasance and the asshole are doing the dirty."

Lisa sighed. "Bastard."

"Uh-huh."

Lisa stepped over the prone form of Famke Jannsen, who would have been livid if she could see what her precious Wolverine was doing over in the corner. "Do we have to clean this mess up? I mean, surely they don't expect the staff—"

"Oh, come on, honey," Angelina interjected. "This is Hollywood Wax we're talking about. We'll have to pick these fucking things up, clean 'em down, take their clothes home and wash them if we have to. Who *else* is gonna do it?"

Lisa rolled her eyes; Angelina was right. This whole mess would have to be cleared up. They'd be pulling wax limbs out of wax asses for the next fortnight.

Lisa crouched and picked up a black arm. "Hey, who's this from?" She glanced around at the celebrity graveyard.

"That's Samuel's," Angelina said. "I think he's over there." She pointed across to the window.

Lisa stood, staggered across more prostrate bodies than a Czech orgy, and made her way to the window, where Samuel L. Jackson looked a little worse for wear. "Sorry about this, Jules," she said as she placed the wax appendage next to him. "I hope it wasn't your masturbating hand."

Just then there was a clicking sound. Lisa straightened up to discover that the window was covered with…*things*.

"What the—"

"What are those things?" Angelina said, stepping tentatively towards the window to get a better look.

"Bugs, I think," Lisa opined. "Are those teeth?"

Angelina tripped over John Travolta's outstretched leg and almost hit the ground. Lisa threw out a hand at the last second, which Angelina latched onto. "Bugs with *teeth*?" Lisa said, hauling her co-worker up.

"Hey, remember that film I made for Troma?

The one with the bugs—"

"That had teeth," Lisa finished the sentence for her. "Yeah, but that was just a shitty movie—"

"Hey!" Angelina yelped. "That movie was one of the better ones I've done."

"I know," Lisa said. "Honey, you need a *real* job."

They stared at the beetles swarming over the glass. Their mouths were filled with jagged, razor-sharp pins; the sound of a thousand legs clicking on the window was almost unbearable.

"I've never seen anything like…" Lisa paused. She clenched Angelina's arm so tight that Angelina's face contorted with pain.

"What? What *is* it?"

"There's something crawling up my leg," Lisa said. Her face portrayed perfect horror the way Angelina had failed to in any of her sixteen roles as an actress.

"Quit fucking around," Angelina said. "Ain't no way those things could get—" It was then that she looked down and saw the beetles skittering across the highly-polished floorboard and over Lisa's shoes. Speckled with marks that gave them something of a clownish appearance, a hundred jolly faces grinned up at her before disappearing up into Lisa's trouser.

Angelina peeled Lisa's hand from her arm and

stepped away. Lisa was paralyzed with fear and could do nothing about her friend's reluctance to be near her. "Just don't make any sudden movements," she said. "I'll go for help."

"Sudden movements," Lisa whispered. "What the fuck *are* they?"

"Shhhh, everything's going to be alright. Just stay here. I'll go get help." She walked cautiously back. Lisa, she could see, was shivering with fear. The bugs – the ones that had managed to somehow get in – were no longer visible, which meant they were up Lisa's trouser-leg, which meant that she had something in the region of a hundred razor-toothed beetles crawling up towards her holiest of holes in that moment.

The thought made Angelina shudder.

"Just. Stay. Calm."

But then Lisa screamed. The most blood-curdling scream Angelina had ever heard, and she spent the majority of her time knocking around B-movie film sets. Her co-worker's eyes were wide, so wide they threatened to drop out and roll across the room. The scream went on, and on, and Lisa began to pat at her clothes as if they were ablaze. Firstly her trousers, then her blouse, and then the bugs emerged from the neck-hole, from the buttons holding the whole thing together. What was once a pure, white blouse was now a crimson blossom. Angelina watched as the beetles scurried through

Lisa's hair and across her face until crawling into her wide-open mouth.

There was nothing for it.

Angelina turned and ran.

*   *   *

Highland Avenue was deserted by the time 'A' Platoon arrived. At least, it was bereft of live people. There were plenty of shiny, red bodies scattered around the vicinity. The moonlight glistened on them, giving them an unreal appearance. The crew were reluctant to leave the apparatus.

"Call base," Joe Myner suggested. "Find out what went on here."

Kyle lifted the radio and glanced out at the abandoned police cars haphazardly strewn across the street. A few of the glistening bodies had remnants of uniform attached to them. Whatever had done this had had no problem in taking down the law. In LA, that was something only gangster-rappers did.

"Base, this is 'A' Platoon. Is Dan there…or some fucker who knows what's going on?"

There was a momentary pause before Dan's voice broke the deafening silence. *"That you,*

Kyle?"

"It's me, Dan. What the hell happened down here?"

"Ask him why we were sent into a fucking warzone!" Luke Vincent whined from the seat behind. Kyle held up a placatory hand. The three crew members sighed in unison and settled back into their seats.

"We don't know what they are...exactly," the division chief said. *"Just that they're dangerous. Very dangerous."*

"Dan, I'm staring out the fucking truck window. Do you know what I can see? Bodies. Everywhere, Dan. More bodies than I've pulled out of fires in my entire fucking career."

"They killed all of them?" Dan said, though it wasn't so much a question as it was a statement.

"Yes, Dan. They – whatever *they* are – killed all of them, whoever *them* are. And you sent us down her to do what, exactly?"

"Shit, I don't know, Kyle." Dan's voice cracked. "I figured the cops down there needed all the help they could get. Sounded pretty chaotic when the call came in."

"Not chaotic at all, now," Kyle replied. "And there's no sign of any flesh-eating bugs, either. I think I'd feel more comfortable knowing where the fuck they were."

"*I* wouldn't," Luke said. "If they're not here,

they're someplace else. That's good enough for me."

"Why don't you get your asses back here?" Dan sighed. "Ain't doing no good sitting out there like tits in the breeze. Just be careful. We're getting calls in from all over. The whole place is teeming with...*what*...?" The division chief broke off as a shrill scream crackled from the radio. Kyle pulled his head away momentarily. The scream faded to a throaty gurgle.

"Dan? Dan, what's going on?" Kyle asked, resuming the communication. "Dan? Do you read me?"

When his voice came next, he sounded breathless, and hurt. "Kyle, they're fucking *everywhere*...don't   come   back here...they're...eating...every—"

The radio began to crackle as if something had gnawed through the cable at the other end. You could have cut the atmosphere in the truck with a rubber spoon. Nobody wanted to be the first to speak, and although Kyle knew he should step up to the plate – they were, after all, his crew, and it was his responsibility to bolster his boys in times of crisis – he didn't want to be held accountable for something he had no fucking idea about.

"Those things a-are at-at the b-base," Freddy Mains said with his trademark stutter working overtime. "Th-they k-killed the ch-chief."

"We don't know that," Kyle said.

"Oh, come on, Kyle," said Joe, leaning over the seat and placing a hand on Kyle's shoulder. "You heard the radio. Sounded a little lively over there, don't you think?"

"Just shut up and let me think for a second."

"Think away, Kyle," Luke said. "In the meantime, we'll sit here and wait for the swarm to return."

"Look, we really need to get a grip here," Joe said. "These things, whatever they are, came right after the quake, right? Is it possible they were lying somewhere, dormant, and the quake woke them up?"

"That's a lovely fairy-tale, Joe," Luke sneered, "but that's not getting us away from all these dead fuckers, is it?"

In the front seat, Kyle rubbed his nose between thumb and forefinger. If he'd only listened to his stupid intuition that morning, all of this might have been avoided. Well, not the quake; that was the kind of thing that was going to happen whether you wanted it to or not. But if he'd just listened to that gut-feeling, he could have called into work sick, took the car and put as much distance as possible between himself and LA. Hindsight was a great thing, and Kyle *had* it, he just didn't have the gumption to do anything about it.

A knock at the window caused all four firefighters to jump back. The man who had knocked made the universally-recognized gesture of "wind the fucking window down".

"Wh-who is this g-guy?" Freddy said, sounding more like a Looney Tunes character with every passing minute.

The man was wearing a brown suit, green shirt and purple tie. It was as if he'd had an accident, swerved into a Goodwill and emerged wearing whatever had hit him on the way through the windshield.

"I don't trust it," Luke said. "He looks too confident."

"He'd have to be to wear that combination," Joe added.

Kyle slowly, cautiously, wound the window halfway. The man smiled and took a deep breath before speaking. "You're probably wondering why I'm standing out here when there's a swarm of hungry Skinners about, aren't you?" he said. The gap in the top row of his teeth was wide enough to put a quarter between with room to spare; Kyle was overcome by the strange urge to stick his finger in it and waggle it about. He wondered whether anyone had actually done it before. Probably...

"Skinners?" Kyle said. "You mean the things that did..." he gestured to the slick, dead corpses lying scattered in the street, "…all *this*?"

"I might know what they are," the man said, glaring nervously around at the carnage, "but that doesn't make me immune to them. I don't suppose there's room in there for one more, is there? I might be able to help."

*   *   *

"And if you look out of the left hand side of the bus right now," the guide said, signalling towards the right as he was relatively new and hadn't come to terms with the concept of mirroring, "you'll see the Walk Of Fame."

The tourists on the right of the open-top bus made their way across to the other side. "I can't see anything," one woman said. Her hat had fruit in it; the guide had originally mistaken her for Lady Gaga. "Can't we get any closer?"

Staring out the front of the bus, the guide said, "Usually, yes, but there are a lot of flashing lights down there tonight. Probably clearing up debris from the tremor. I think it's best if we skip this part of the tour."

"I want to see the Walk of Fame," a child said, tugging her father's hand like the brat from "Charlie and The Chocolate Factory." *Daddy, I want a party with roomfuls of laughter, ten thousand tons of ice-*

cream, and if I don't get the things I am after, I'm going to screeeeaaAAAAMMMMM.

The father, a rotund sonofabitch if ever the guide saw one, said, "We've paid for this tour, and we want the whole thing. Not just snippets."

"I appreciate that," said the guide, "but the street's blocked by police cars. You honestly want to get closer? Put that darling of yours in danger?"

The man glanced down at his daughter, who was giving him her best impression of a Furby. "I don't want to go if there's a chance of being shot or falling into a crack," she said.

"Wise words," the guide said. "This is LA. You're more likely to die from a gunshot wound than die of natural causes." He radioed down to the driver, informed him that it was best to continue along Vine and forget about the Walk tonight.

"Ladies and gentlemen, please return to your seats," the guide said. "We'll be moving on with the tour now, and I wouldn't want—"

"What's that?" Lady Gaga asked, pointing a spindly, heavily-manicured finger down the avenue. The bus creaked and rocked as tourists made their way over to see what she was talking about.

Something was approaching the bus. At first it looked like liquid; its fluidity made Gaga think of semen, a whole sea of it heading for the bus where it would impregnate her with twins, triplets, fucking *quads*. The mere thought of it made her fruity hat topple from her head, revealing a beehive of epic proportions.

"Are those mice?" the little girl asked. Her father shook his fat face; he had no idea what they were.

"Listen," the guide said. "Everyone just calm down and remain seated."

The swarm reached the bus and began to chirrup and screech, as if they were aware of the feast gazing down, confused, from the upper deck.

"They're bugs!" Gaga screamed. "They're dirty, rotten bugs and they're climbing the side of the bus." She stood and barged her way through the enraptured throng to get to the empty side of the bus. "I hate bugs!"

"Holy shit!" an old lady roared from the back of the bus. It was the kind of roar that suggested she hadn't always been an old lady, that she had once been able to pitch a perfect inning in the Dixie Boys' league. "They look like clowns!" She finished her sentence just as the creatures began to pour over the side of the bus, their incessant chattering enough to drive anyone insane. The old lady – *Derrick* – was instantly swamped by the creatures. As they swallowed her entirely, her false teeth shot from her screaming mouth and landed in the middle of the bus.

The tourists began to scream and rush for the

stairs. Big mistake. Veruca Salt's father – he of the generous waistline – managed to wedge his sizeable frame between the floors, leaving all those unfortunate enough to be on the upper-deck with nowhere to run. The geriatric ladyboy at the rear of the bus was nothing more than bones and tendon; she slumped to the floor with a meaty thump, as bugs scattered across the upper-deck.

Gaga threw her legs over the side of the bus and began to slowly lower herself. She hadn't given it much thought, but the ten-inch heels she wore would almost guarantee two broken ankles when she hit the tarmac. She flicked them off, took a deep breath, and was about to jump when something scrambled across her right hand, then her left. She felt a momentary sting on her knuckles before she let go and began her descent towards the street. Landing better than she would have if she'd kept the stilts on, she rolled once and struggled to her knees.

She checked her knuckles, and was surprised to find that there weren't any. Her hand was possessed of a perfectly hollow stripe from the intermediate phalange to the metacarpals. Of course, she didn't know the terms for the bones that were now visible. All she knew was that she was going to upchuck.

She didn't get the opportunity. The terrible sensation of something crawling over her legs, up her back, and over her neck prevented her from doing anything except let out one final, hellish squeal. Her beehive fell onto the tarmac in front of her as the creatures removed her scalp like miniature lawnmowers. Blood dribbled down into her eyes, sticking them instantly together so that she didn't have to witness the terrible things that followed.

She felt it, though.

Every. Last. Second.

*   *   *

"Everyone, I'm afraid we're going to have to close the bar for tonight. If you could make your way slowly and safely towards the exits, we'd be much obliged."

There was a collective sigh and grumble of disapproval around the Hard Rock Café as the realisation of a premature end to the revellers' night finally hit home. Spike wanted nothing more than to announce the continuation of the festivities, but the damage from the quake was too severe. There were broken bottles and shards of jagged glass everywhere. To simply ignore the mess would be crazy; he might as well take down the names and addresses of those present as they left the bar just to make the lawsuits easier to handle.

Drunken, crestfallen people staggered for the doors at the front of the building. The acrid stench of stale beer was pungent enough to cause eyes to water.

"Hey, Spike," Lindsey called across the sticky, battered bar. "Does that mean I get to go home?"

Spike ran his fingers through his long, dark hair. "Wouldn't that make me the nicest boss ever?" he said sardonically. Lindsey's jaw dropped so low that it almost touched the beer-drenched counter.

Tonight should have been a real earner for the place; across town, Thick Lizzy was playing. As one of the better tribute acts on the scene, they had promised Spike that the aftershow party would take place at his bar. He'd counted on at least two-hundred extra heads, which would have meant an extra couple thousand in revenue.

And then there had been a quake...

Of *course* there fucking had. It was just Spike's luck, and now he had a bar to clean, and that bitch Lindsey was giving him the evil-eye from across the room, which meant he would have to suffer her indefatigable whining for the remainder of the night. The shit hadn't just hit the fan; it had bounced off and splattered him in the face.

As the room emptied, Spike cracked open a beer and leaned, dejectedly, against the counter. Lindsey clattered around with a brush; Spike wondered if it was her time of the month, but didn't have the nerve to ask her.

There were roughly thirty people still trying to leave the bar when, suddenly, they began to push back. Outside on the street, women were screaming, and men were yelling in guttural tones that suggested a fight had broken out.

Spike slammed his beer down on the counter. "Now what the hell…"

The people still in the bar toppled back, crushed by the reversing crowd from outside. It was like a gigantic game of pile-on, or some weird, fully-clothed orgy that would never get off the ground.

The writhing, screaming bodies were suddenly blanketed by thousands of white…*things*. All it took was five seconds. Hands punched up through the creatures; bloodied, skinned fists trying to break free of the madness. The screams of the people beneath the swarm were muted, somewhat, by the intolerable chirping of the bugs.

"We're gonna need a bigger bar," Spike said, realising how silly it sounded the moment it passed his lips. Brody he wasn't.

To his left, Lindsey was trying to brush away the encroaching insects as if they were peanuts. They crawled up the brush-handle and within seconds, she was as white as a ghost while the beetles swallowed her completely.

Spike, finally able to move, raced for the cellar door. As he reached it, he turned to see the swarm slip away from the pile of bodies to reveal a huge, steaming pile of remains. It looked like something out of a bad horror flick, something from an Angelina Frost movie.

"Hasta la vista, baby," Spike said in broken Austrian, before slamming the door to the cellar, sliding the bolt across and disappearing down into the darkness.

*   *   *

Walking into Lucky Strike Lanes was like stumbling into an abattoir. A pile of skinned corpses were stacked erroneously at the door; the flayed remains of the unfortunate bastards who had tried to escape the bugs. It was impossible to tell how many dead were in the mound without stopping to count limbs. Tom and Mike had entered through the back door, since the front was so adroitly obstructed.

"Poor fuckers," Mike said, gazing over the pile of bone and viscera. "To think they only came out for a game of—"

"Never mind all that," Tom interrupted like the heartless sonofabitch he was. "We need to make sure those things are all gone and barricade the back doors. For all we know those things can fucking smell flesh. They might come back."

Mike hadn't thought about it, but now that Tom had mentioned it his skin crawled. He slapped at his neck.

"What?" Tom said, checking the director over.

Mike scratched his head. "Nothing. I just had an itch, that's all."

Tom walked along the carpet at the end of the alleys. A few people had been peeled mid-bowl. The only remaining skin on them was pushed into the three holes of the balls in the shape of a thumb and two fingers. At the end of the hall – Alley 20 – there must have been a tournament-game in progress; two teams had been savagely stripped of their colours (and skin) by those insidious beetles. The earthquake must have been nothing more than a tremor in the bowling alley as half-finished glasses of beer were perched precariously upon tables.

"Do you think we're safe here?" Mike asked, still raking at his neck as if under attack from invisible, infinitesimal bugs.

Tom shrugged. He was trying to find something to barricade the back doors with, even though he didn't believe the beetles – *Clown faces? Why the fuck did they look so goddamn jolly?* – could break down doors or push over blockades. They were smart, though, and able to fit through even the tiniest aperture.

Lucky Strike Lanes was filled with small holes; it was practically impossible to cover them all. Keeping those things at bay was like trying to stop water from running through a colander.

Still, it didn't hurt to try. Tom grabbed the end of a cabinet and tipped it, spilling smelly shoes across the carpet. "Help me with this," he said. Mike walked across and took the other end of the cabinet.

They carried it to the back and placed it strategically in front of the exit. The front was already blocked, thanks to the mountain of indiscernible cadavers. Unless there was another door, Tom figured they had it pretty much covered.

"So now what?" Mike asked. "We just sit tight and wait for the army?"

Tom snorted. "What's the army gonna do about those fucking things, Mike?" He peeled open a bag of peanuts and began to toss them into his mouth. As he continued to speak, flecks of nut flew here, there, and everywhere. Mike stepped back; he was allergic to nuts and now was not the time or place for anaphylaxis. "Those things are unstoppable. They're too fast and there're too damn many of 'em. If the army sends their boys down here, they're just gonna end up dead like the rest of us."

"We ain't dead, yet," Mike said. "And I don't plan on dying anytime soon. I'm contracted to make six pictures next year."

"Oh, I'm sure if you explain that to the bugs, they'll let you live. I've heard they're partial to mindless action movies."

"Maybe this is a sign," Mike said, dragging a stool towards him. Sitting, he continued, "Maybe *Lethal Agent IV* was never meant to be made."

Tom almost choked on the nuts in his overfilled mouth. He coughed, swallowed, then said, "What the fuck is *that* supposed to mean? What, just 'cos I'm not the highest grossing actor anymore? Those films have made you rich, you ungrateful bastard. You should just be glad that my agent talked me into doing them in the first place. I turned down *Macbeth* for you, you fucker."

"*Macbeth*, Tom?" Mike sneered. "Really?"

"I was a *real* actor before the studios realised I'd make more money throwing myself from trains. As soon as they knew I wasn't afraid to do my own stunts, that was it. No more offers for serious roles; Tom Harker only gets the meathead parts." He exhaled, both air and peanuts. "Do you know how frustrating it is when my agent calls? I always hope he's got me something decent, something…*award-worthy*."

"What was that one where you played the president? People who play presidents are usually noted actors."

"Mike, that was *Abraham Lincoln, Mummy*

Catcher. Hardly gonna get an Oscar for that one, am I?"

"Good movie," Mike muttered.

"Look, I need a piss. Check around the place, will you. There's got to be something here we can use if those things come back." He tossed the empty peanut-wrapper to the floor and headed across the hall.

"Oh, Tom," Mike said, remembering something important he'd been meaning to ask. Tom turned. "Why did we come here? You picked this place over all the other slaughterhouses."

Tom shrugged. "I thought somebody might have come here." He pointed to the mound of corpses at the entrance. "For all I know, she *did*." He turned and headed towards the shitter.

*   *   *

There were, Spike realized, only so many hours you could spend in complete, silent darkness before madness began to set in. Aside from the fact that it had all gone quiet up in the bar, he was curious to see if anyone had survived the bugs' assault. As a kid, he'd been locked, cruelly, in a cupboard beneath the stairs for almost a whole day. His so-called friends had thought it was the funniest thing ever; Spike had been claustrophobic for years after. This reminded him a little of that, only it wasn't his sniggering friends out there, it was evil clown-faced beetles.

There wasn't that much difference between the two, after all.

He slowly made his way up the cellar steps, listening carefully for any sudden noises on the other side of the door.

"Everybody just stay calm, the situation is under control," he whispered to himself. It was another movie quote. Some days, he only spoke in quotes. It drove the staff crazy, especially Lindsey.

He paused on the steps. The darkness made it easier to think about what had happened up there, how those things had swarmed over Lindsey, how she had been trying to brush them away like an idiot. It was a shame, really. She wasn't all bad, Spike thought. He continued up the steps in the pitch black, not knowing what he was about to discover, and for once not giving a shit about the mess of the Hard Rock Café.

*　　*　　*

It felt good to piss. Tom was surprised he'd managed to hold it in while people had been getting stripped of their skin; that was the kind of thing that usually resulted in an accidental urination.

When he was done, he shook twice. The voice of his dead mother reminded him that any more than twice and he was playing with it.

He zipped himself up and turned from the urinal. Pain coursed through his body and his legs gave way beneath him. As he landed on the piss-drenched tiles beneath, he realised someone had hit him – *hard* – around the head.

"Tom?" a slightly fuzzy voice said. "Shit, Tom, I'm sorry!"

He glanced up from the discomfort of the toilet floor, and once the room stopped spinning he realised that the person who'd clobbered him was, in fact, Angelina Frost.

She grabbed him beneath the arms and tried to pick him up. His head was cut up pretty bad from where the U-bend section had impacted; blood dripped slowly down past his ear, though she doubted it would make any severe alterations to his personality.

Composing himself as best he could, Tom glowered at the Goth girl. "What the fuck did you hit me for?"

"Shit, Tom, I've been hiding in that cubicle for hours. For all I knew you were a rapist."

Tom patted at the wound on his head, hissing through his teeth. "Typical," he said. "As soon as the world shows any signs of ending, all men are instantly rapists and barbarians." He snatched the piece of piping from her. "And quit swinging that around like Xena, will you? You're making me nervous."

"How did you know I'd be here?" Angelina asked as she pulled paper-towels from the dispenser. "I thought those...*things* got you."

He accepted the towels she offered him and began to dab the dribbling cut at the side of his head. "We were supposed to meet here at twelve, remember?" he said. "We were filming a scene when the quake hit, and then those fucking bugs came out of nowhere."

"I was at the museum," Angelina said. "They got Lisa and everyone else. I made it out onto the street, but they were everywhere." She paused at the thought of so many innocent people being slaughtered. "I saw one of the Hollywood Sign tours get attacked," she said. "One minute people were staring through telescopes, the next they were covered in bugs."

"Clowns..." Tom mumbled.

"They *do* look like clowns, don't they?" She shuddered. "It was as if God had been trying to come up with the creepiest thing imaginable. Bugs and clowns, together at last." She sniggered, though it seemed forced.

"Yeah," Tom said. "It was either that or spider-mimes."

"Now that *would* be creepy," she said. "Look, Tom, I don't know how we're going to get through this. If those creatures get in he—"

"Look, you leave that up to me," Tom sad, grabbing her by the shoulders. "I won't let anything bad happen to you." He knew he was lying; he couldn't help it. Stick a pretty girl in front of him, and the chance of one last fuck before the end of days, and all manner of shit was liable to fall from his lips.

She leaned in to hug him; he reluctantly returned the gesture. "I just hope the army gets here soon."

What is it with people thinking the army is gonna come? Tom thought.

"I'm sure they're on their way as we speak." *There you go again, Tom. You're going straight to hell.* Not that hell could be any worse than LA at that particular moment in time.

*   *   *

Sherman Kessler was squashed on the back seat between Joe and Luke. Freddy Mains had refused to sit by him, said he had a strange smell, like liquorice and bath-salts. "Never trust a man that smells like bath-salts," Freddy had whispered to Kyle, though he'd stuttered the shit out if it.

"So what you're saying is that this isn't the first time this has happened?" Kyle said. "The government knows about these things, and they're quite content to let them pop up every now and again to say hello? Is that it?"

Sherman shuffled uncomfortably in the rear. "Not the government, no. At least, not all of it." He freed his arm from Joe Myner's considerable weight before proceeding. "I was hired by a private company a few years ago. I'm an entomologist, and I—"

"What, like Houdini?" Luke said, interrupting the geek mid-flow.

"I don't...what...that means...oh you mean an *escapologist*. No, nothing like that. Entomology is the study of insects. My job was to research and catalogue the behaviour and biomechanics of beetles. The company that hired me knew I was the best in my field, and so it was no surprise that I was soon running the entire department—"

"Skip to the end," Kyle interrupted. He'd taken the truck around the block three times already and they were still no wiser as to what the fucking things were.

Sherman, slightly perturbed by the driver's brusque tone, said, "They are the descendants of a very, very old species of beetle. One of the oldest this earth has ever known. We at the lab like to call them *Fossor Scarabaeus*—"

"In En-English, p-please," Freddy said.

"It translates as Clown Beetle," Sherman said. "You'll see what I mean when you get up close and personal with one."

"Ain't gonna happen if we can help it," Luke said. "Right, boss?"

Kyle didn't know what to say, so he ignored the question altogether. "You said this isn't the first time?"

"It's the first time in such a populated area," Sherman said, becoming excited at the prospect of another overlong explanation. "Out in the desert they're always surfacing. That's where we do most of our research. There was a pretty severe case a few years back in Connecticut. A whole swarm of *Fossor Scarabaeus* popped up on a golf course in Hartford, killed George Bush Junior and his entire entourage right in the middle of the fifteenth hole."

"Bullshit!" Kyle said, steering hard to the right. "Bush is still alive."

Sherman leaned forward in his seat. "That ain't been the real Bush since 2007. Hard to believe, I know. How could they possibly replicate all that charm and swagger?"

"W-why w-would they e-even bother?" Freddy asked.

"People don't like to hear that their president has been skinned alive by prehistoric beetles," Sherman said. "It's bad for morale."

"So if this isn't a new thing, there's got to be some sort of insecticide, something that can kill these things." Kyle pulled the truck over; the gauge was flickering orange, which meant they were almost out of fuel. There was no point wasting what remained by riding round the block again.

"They're nothing special," Sherman said. "They can be killed by any normal insecticide, but the quantities we're talking to take care of such a vast swarm…"

"Go on," Joe urged.

"I don't think any of us expected LA to have to deal with an attack on this scale. We'd need gallons of insecticide, barrels of it, and even then I'm not sure it would make a difference."

"We have to do something," Kyle said.

"We could pump it through the hoses," Luke added; his grin suggested he was more than satisfied with his proposition. "Yeah, just shoot the little fuckers where they feed. That could work, couldn't it?"

Sherman Kessler thought about it. "It might do," he said, "but there's no way we could get that amount of killer in time. You've seen how quickly those things feed; half the city'll be skinned by now."

Just then, a woman pushing a trolley rushed in front of the truck. Skinners were all over her. There was barely a morsel left on her, and yet she reluctantly clung to the trolley as if the possessions contained within would somehow save her…eventually. As she sauntered on, screeching as the bugs relieved her of her nose, the firefighters shook their heads in unison.

"So let's not waste any more fucking time disputing it," Kyle said, putting the truck into gear and hoping they had enough fuel to get them wherever they needed to be. "You're the expert; where's the nearest place we can get insecticide from?"

"We have it at the lab," Sherman said. He didn't sound as enthusiastic as he could have. "Maybe enough to take out a few hundred of them, anyway."

"Direct me," Kyle said as he began to drive. "A few hundred less of those clown motherfuckers is a good place to start."

*   *   *

They fed, and fed, and just when they thought they were full, along came another bunch of unassuming humans, and they fed some more. By now, they were bloated so much their bellies dragged along the ground. Some of them were beached upon curbs; some of them had rolled onto their backs where they would remain until they were knocked back the right way up, or until the digested flesh left their system.

This particular swarm rested. They had got lucky, first with the tour bus and then the Hard Rock Café. That kind of feed was bound to lie heavy on the stomach, and like most creatures, the quickest and most efficient way of digesting food was to get a few hours of sleep.

There was a nice, dark hole at the side of one building, and thousands of the bugs had wedged themselves into it. They couldn't read the flashing, neon sign hanging over the gloomy recess.

Lucky Strike Lanes.

For now they slept, if only to fill the gap until they could feed once again.

*   *   *

Spike wandered through the night. The rain peppering him made him wish he'd put on his leather jacket. Inclement weather, though, had been the last thing on his mind when he left the bar. Outside was much the same as the hell he'd just left behind. Everywhere he turned, there were corpses.

He was, truth be told, terrified of straying too far from the bar, despite his desire to leave behind that grisly stack of stripped cadavers. If the bugs attacked, he wanted to be able to get back to his cellar in one piece. The pool cue in his hand wasn't going to do much to protect him, not if he stumbled across a swarm the size of the one that had attacked his punters back at the bar.

What in the hell *were* those things?

He hadn't seen one up close and personal – it wasn't on his bucket-list, either – but he knew a beetle when he saw one.

But he'd never seen so many all packed into one place, and he'd certainly never seen one rend the flesh from a living person before.

"Fucking monsters," he muttered quietly.

That's exactly what they were, he thought. Some government experiment gone awry, or bacteria from another world come to earth via a meteor, or satellite, or fucking space-junk…

Something scrabbled in an alleyway to Spike's right. He stopped walking, fearful that his footfall would alert whatever was down there to his presence. Then he glanced around and realised he was standing out in the open. If there was something down there, and it came out into the street, the first thing it would see would be the man shaking like a shitting dog in the middle of the road with a pool cue raised above his head.

He quickly made his way over to the side of the street, being careful not to kick any of the debris that littered the sidewalk.

Do beetles have ears? Shit, why didn't I pay more attention in Biology?

It didn't matter though, did it? These weren't ordinary beetles; these were space-beetles from the planet Clownanus. They probably had radars instead of ears, and eyes that could smell, and…*well*, he knew very well what their teeth looked like. He'd watched them strip the meat away from Lindsey – poor, angry Lindsey – like she was a bargain-bucket. They had rows and rows of needle-sharp teeth. *All the better to eat you with, my dear.*

Spike pushed himself between two cars and waited. Whatever was down the alleyway would either show itself, or…it *wouldn't*. Then what? He wasn't just going to stand there all night, the meat in a Prius sandwich. And the pool-cue was about as useful as a one-legged man in an ass-kicking contest; he may as well have been holding his dick, for all the good it would do him.

Another clatter came from the alley. Spike shrank as much as he possibly could, not that it would do any good against their heat-seeking missiles or super-sensitive night-vision. The latter was possible, he guessed as he discarded the thought of flying bombs.

Then it walked nonchalantly out onto the street. A cat. A stupid, fucking cat. Spike exhaled. He hadn't even realised he'd been holding his breath, but if he had a mirror handy he would have seen the strange shade of purple he had turned.

The cat ambled into the road, patting at a tile on the ground as if it were something living.

Spike stepped out from the cars and continued along the street. The cat followed him suspiciously for a while before disappearing off into the darkness of another alleyway. Spike was disappointed when it left. He named it Lindsey, after the last pussy that got away.

*   *   *

Mike, Tom and Angelina stood by the bar. Mike made them cocktails; it seemed silly not to. Angelina was sipping from something green, while Tom and Mike considered the unappetizing-looking liquid in their own glasses. It looked like bile, or something you would find inside a killer whale. Tom placed his glass down on the counter and began to rummage around in his jacket pocket.

"What are you looking for?" Mike asked, realizing there was no way he was drinking the luminous green shit he'd made moments earlier. He put his glass down next to Tom's.

Tom pulled out a cell phone. "Maybe we can call somebody?" he said, jabbing viciously at the keypad. After a few seconds, he growled, "*Fuck*! No bars."

It was amazing it had taken this long for any of them to consider calling for help; Mike took out his own cell and switched it on. The welcoming tone of some ancient Beyoncé tune broke the nervous silence. When Mike glanced up he found Angelina and Tom sniggering.

"What?" Mike said, trying not to appear embarrassed by his choice of music. "'Single Ladies' is a great fucking song."

"If you're a nine year-old girl," Angelina said. "Shit, we're in real trouble here."

"Now, now," Tom said, stifling a snigger. "I'm sure Mike, like every normal man, just wants to bang her."

Mike shook his head. "Doesn't do anything for me. Her music's *great*, though." He held the phone aloft, as if offering it to the gods. Keeping his eye on the signal, or lack thereof, in the corner of the screen, he said, "Nope, nothing here, either."

"Of *course* we're not gonna get a signal," Angelina said, wiping green drool from her bottom lip. Tom found it somewhat erotic – like maybe she'd just given Shrek a blowjob – but didn't say anything. "We're in the middle of a bad horror movie. I'll bet all the phones are down. And why stop *there*? Why don't we split up? Go looking for fuck-knows-what in the dark? I could take my top off, just to make sure that I die next, and—"

"I like that idea," Mike said. Tom clouted him, hard, across the arm. "Ow, *what*? She was offering to disrobe."

"Do *you* have a phone?" Tom asked Angelina. He knew she did; he'd been sending her pictures of his dick for weeks.

"Sure, back at the museum," she replied. "You want me to go fetch it, bring it back here so we can all stare at the blank screen?"

"Shit!" Tom spat. "This is ridiculous." He stopped; apparently deep in thought. After a few moments, he asked, "What if one of us went outside?"

"And there it is," Angelina chided. "The worst goddamn suggestion possible. Hey, if you see a token black guy out there, be sure to let him in. They'll go after him first—"

"Tom's right," Mike said. "We might get a signal out there. I mean, this place is probably soundproofed, or something. But outside, we should be able to get something. At least a couple of bars, just enough to call for help."

"Do any of you have the number of a good

exterminator?" asked Angelina. She was really starting to get on Tom's tits. "Because, if you didn't already notice, the LAPD have been chewed up and spat out. You think that people don't know what's going on here? They know, and they're just letting it happen. Those fucking clown-bugs can't be beaten, or destroyed, or tamed. They can't be trained to not eat us and packaged for little Emily to open on Christmas morning. They're just gonna keep coming until everyone's dead, all of us. I'll bet the lack of signal has nothing to do with where we are; it's been switched the fuck off by whoever's in charge."

"We don't know any of that," Tom said, "so keep your conspiracy theories to yourself. Shit, anytime something bad happens all the David Ickes come crawling out the woodwork."

Angelina shrugged. "Well, why don't one of you retarded pricks go take a walk outside, huh? Maybe you'll get through to the Ghostbusters." She turned and launched the half-empty glass of bile across the room where it smashed against an Elvis Presley pinball machine. "By the way, Mike, you make shitty cocktails."

Mike nodded. "Agreed. Now, we need to figure out which one of us is—"

"You," Tom said, cutting Mike off mid-sentence.

"Me?" Mike said. "Why *me*?"

Tom gasped, feigning shock. "Do you know who I am? Oh, oh, of *course* you do. You want to put me at risk, one of America's greatest actors? *Huh*? Do you think Spielberg's somewhere right now trying to push Tom Hanks out into the street?"

"Tom, you're not Tom Hanks, though, are you? Or Tom Hardy, or—"

"Oliver Hardy," Angelina added. "Though this is another fine mess you've got us into."

"Keep cracking jokes, scream-queen," Tom said, bitterly. "At least I don't have titty-scenes written into my contract."

"You *should*," Angelina said. "Those bitch-tits of yours are really something."

"Look, this isn't helping," Mike said. "And you know what? *I'll* do it, and not because I'm worried about putting you at risk, Tom. You're just like the rest of us to those things. Meat…*flesh*…something they'll be picking out of their teeth at the end of the night if one of us doesn't do something, and fast."

Tom, for the first time since they'd barricaded the doors, was dumbstruck and relieved. The last thing he wanted to do was put himself at the mercy of the beetles. And Mike was a good guy – a shit director, but a good guy – for stepping up when he didn't have to.

"You only have to go outside," Tom told him. "If there's no bars you get your ass back in as quickly as possible. We don't want those things knowing we're in here."

"We'll be right by the door," Angelina said. Tom shot her a glance that suggested he wasn't pleased with that idea. "What? We need to be able to let him back in, don't we?"

"That would be nice," Mike sneered.

"Of course we'll be by the door," Tom said. *By the door, ready to lock your fat ass out if any of those fucking things turn up!* "If you manage to get a signal, you call whoever you can."

"I wouldn't bother with the police," Angelina said. "From what I saw on the way over here, there aren't many left."

So Ghostbusters it is, Mike thought.

"Let's do this, then," Tom said. "Fucking clown-beetles. Who'd have thought it?"

* * *

The lab was on Franklin Avenue. From the outside it looked like apartments; the kind of place the government put poor people to forget about them. At the side of the building there was a large, white industrial gate with a No Entry sign hanging on it – the only suggestion that this was a place of work.

Sherman squeezed his way past the firemen and out of the truck, where he proceeded to unlock the gate with a set of keys chained to his belt. When the gate was unlocked, he motioned to Kyle to drive forward.

"Are we taking orders from this geek, now?" Luke muttered.

"He might be the only chance we have," Kyle said.

"My mother always warned me about talking to men who wore purple," said Joe.

"Well, we don't really have much choice, do we?" Kyle replied, pulling the truck over to allow Sherman back in.

They drove down an incline, and before they knew it they were beneath the building. Several cars were parked in allocated spaces.

"People working overtime?" Kyle asked.

"Not likely," Sherman said. "These cars are always down here; have been for years. They belong to people who've died while working for BioTex. It's kind of like a homage to them to keep the cars around."

"A fucking graveyard's what it is," Luke said. "I mean, who *does* that?"

Sherman directed Kyle through the underground maze of dead men's cars. "This is it," he said. Kyle pulled the truck over and they all climbed out.

"Don't suppose there's any food in there?" Joe

asked, stretching like a cat recently roused from slumber. "Feels like days since I ate."

"It's been two hours," Kyle said. "You'd make a shit Jew."

"I could fucking *eat* a Jew," Joe said. "Hey, Sherman, I don't suppose you're Jewish, are you?" He snapped his teeth together with a click; Sherman made a noise that sounded like a mouse being run over.

"Point the way, Sherman," Kyle said. "We've got a city to save."

The lab was lined with creatures in cages. In fact, you could have charged kids to come down and play with the animals, there were that many. Though parents might not be comfortable letting little Charlie play with a two-headed rat.

"This is not a nice place you've got here, Sherman," Joe said. "No wonder you try to keep it top-secret."

"Well, it has to be done, I'm afraid," the purple-tied geek sighed. "If people knew we were here, there'd be protesters lining the streets, waving their anti-cruelty banners and chanting about how bugs are people, too." He led them along a corridor, past a whole menagerie of mutant creatures. One cage seemed to be home to a giant maggot. The size of a corn-snake, but twice as thick, it looked like something Lorena Bobbitt could go to town on for days.

The door at the end of the corridor led to a smaller room, a room that Sherman announced as, "My office."

"You k-keep the in-insecticide in y-your of-office?" Freddy said.

"Hey, you never know when there's gonna be an outbreak." He walked across the room to a green tarpaulin. "I just hope we have enough." He whipped the tarp away to reveal at least fifteen large containers of Buzz-Kill. "This works best on bees, wasps and hornets," he said, "but I'm pretty sure it'll have the desired effects on the Skinners."

"Pretty sure?" Kyle said, crouching to read the label. It was all written in an ancient language that Kyle was familiar with: gibberish. Scientific bullshit; lots of six-syllable words ending in –*osis*…

"As sure as I can be," Sherman said. "I don't know how long it'll take to work, but if we give them a good spray with this, I think it's safe to say they won't be feeling none too clever come sun-up."

"We need to get this into the truck," Kyle said. "This won't burn through the hoses, will it?"

Sherman shrugged. "Hmmm. Doubtful, but I guess we've never had to shoot it from fire-trucks before."

"Reassuring," Kyle said. "Joe, Luke, start loading—"

He stopped. Somewhere, something was making a strange sound. The high-pitched chirruping almost sounded like crickets. Kyle got to his feet and listened.

"Wh-what i-is that?" Freddy asked.

Sherman's expression faltered. He'd heard that sound before, back in '93, his last encounter with the Skinners. A small swarm had emerged from an old lady's bidet in Lick Skillet, Tennessee. Luckily, the lady hadn't been rinsing her asshole at the time, and the whole thing had been over before it began. Sherman had arrived to discover the old hag had hairsprayed the living shit out of the three bugs; they were stuck solid, and coated with a fine, white mist, but they were still alive, and still making that noise. *Help us! This crazy-ass bitch sprayed us stiff!*

Kyle noticed the fear as it crept over Sherman Kessler's wiry features. He looked as if he'd just been told he couldn't play *World Of Warcraft* ever again.

"Skinners?" Kyle whispered.

Ti-ti-ti-ti-ti-ti-ti-ti-ti, went thousands of tiny legs as they scrambled along the corridor.

Sherman nodded. "Skinners," he said, trying not to sound as if he was about to shit his pants, and failing. He was already attempting to peel the lid off one of the Buzz-Kill containers when all hell broke loose in the lab. Hundreds of them, with their jolly, harlequin motifs, skittered in from the corridor, covering everything they could find.

"H-h-help," said Freddy Mains as the Skinners scampered over him.

"KILL THEM ALL!" Kyle roared, tearing the lid from one container of Buzz-Kill.

It was, unfortunately, much too late to help Freddy, who was now standing *sans* skin. The creatures dropped from him, bellies already distended, and rushed towards Joe and Luke, who were trapped against Sherman's full-size cardboard cut-out of Sarah Michelle Gellar. A few of the bugs proved they weren't intelligent by gnawing their way through the vampire-slayer's thin, tasteless body.

"Get out of the corner!" Kyle yelled, but it was too late. The swarm had finished with *Buffy* and were in need of something more substantial – or at least genuine – to slake their undying hunger. Kyle threw the contents of the container across the room; blue liquid flew through the air, landing short of its target. A few bugs, still crawling along the ground, began to sizzle and melt, leaving behind a black, sticky ichor as they continued towards the cornered firefighters.

Next to Kyle, Sherman was still struggling to get the lid off his container. Kyle snatched it from him and peeled it off with one, mighty heave.

Bugs began to swamp Joe and Luke, who were

flailing around as if they were on fire.

It's because they saw what happened to Freddy! They know they're about to get skinned!

Kyle couldn't let it happen. Freddy was still alive – for now – and standing in the middle of the office as if he was expecting a bus to arrive at any moment. He twitched, probably a result of his nerve-endings being exposed completely. Kyle rushed past him; there was nothing he could do to help him.

Luke dropped to the ground and began to roll. It was a technique they were taught to douse flames, but Luke obviously thought it would work on evil clown-beetles, too. And it did, for the most part; bugs were crushed beneath him, leaving splotches of tarry gunk wherever they died. Luke was still being bitten, and his screams verified that it was hurting like a motherfucker.

Joe wasn't so fortunate. His head was covered with them; Kyle saw twenty, thirty, forty disappear down his shirt where they would peel him apart in seconds.

Kyle threw half the container over Luke, who rolled over onto his back just as one of the beetles tore his eye from its socket and began to carry it away. It didn't get far, though, as the Buzz-Kill began to work. It sizzled, smoked, and began to melt – as did the rest of the creatures swarming Luke.

Kyle turned to find that Sherman had managed to open a container of his own. He was pouring it over Joe Miner's head as if they were part of some comedy duo. As the bugs melted away from Joe's face, though, Kyle knew his friend would never get the chance to thank the geek for his heroism.

"Fuck!" Kyle said, swallowing down the bile that rose in his throat. "This is a nightmare! A fucking nightmare!"

Joe toppled backwards, his cheek flapping loosely against his face. Most of his teeth were exposed, giving him a skeletal appearance. The bugs in his clothing were mostly dead, but Kyle could hear the annoying chittering as a lucky few continued to feed.

Something latched onto Kyle's leg. He looked down, expecting a new swarm to be crawling up his leg, but it was Luke's hand, skinned and bleeding all over the office floor. One beetle had embedded itself between the knuckles, its teeth buried so deep that even as it dissolved, even as the chemicals burned through its shell, it continued to gorge.

"There's nothing we can do for them," Sherman said, dropping his empty container to the floor. "We need to grab what we can and get the hell out of here. There will be more of them."

Kyle stepped away from his dying friend's grasp. "I'm going to kill every last one of them," he said. "I don't care what happens to me; those fuckers don't know what they've started."

"Then let's get the Buzz-Kill to the truck," Sherman said, "and take the war to them."

Kyle nodded, said a prayer for his skinless friends, and loaded as much insecticide onto the truck as he could. The night was going to get ugly.

Very fucking ugly.

*   *   *

"**I**'m pretty sure there's nothing out there," Tom said, glancing through the tiny crack in the back door. He was loath to open it any further just in case he was mistaken. "You're good to go, man."

Mike took a deep breath. "Are you sure, Tom? I mean, those things are pretty small. And *quick*, too."

"The street's clear," Angelina said from the side. She clearly wasn't in the mood for any pussyfooting around. "Either you're going to do it, or not. If not, can you do us all a favour, Tom, and shut the fucking door?"

"Okay," Mike said, jumping up and down, nervously shaking his hands as if he was about to take part in some Olympic event. He didn't look fit enough to walk to the end of the street.

"What's all that?" Tom asked. "Mike, you're

only stepping outside for a minute. I doubt whether you need to do a full warm-up."

"Look, I'm doing it, aren't I? Just stop talking for a second."

Tom and Angelina smiled at each other. "Just go as far as the bins," Angelina said. "There's nothing there that could block the signal. If you're gonna get anything, that's where it will happen."

Mike suddenly wished he hadn't opened his big mouth back in the hall. This was his idea; if anyone deserved to die, it was him for making such a ridiculous suggestion. So what if they got a signal? He had three numbers in his phone: his doctor, his mother, and his ex-wife. He wasn't certain, but surely if they had crazy clown-bug-killing experience they would have mentioned it before now. Though his ex-wife was pretty good at keeping secrets – as she'd proved with the mailman – he wouldn't be surprised to find out she was queen of the Bug Assassinator's Guild.

The bins, as Mike stared out at them, looked an awful way off.

"Okay, I'm gonna do this," he said. He took one final, deep breath as Tom stepped aside, opening the door just enough for Mike to squeeze his rotund frame through.

If there are any clown-beetles out there, Tom thought, *they're in for one hell of a meal.*

Mike felt the rain on his balding pate; hundreds of icy needles jabbing at the place where there had once been hair.

A long, long, time ago.

He clenched the phone tightly in his right hand. Any tighter and it would have crumbled into useless pieces.

Perhaps that was what he subconsciously hoped for. No phone meant no sacrifice; Mike could turn around and head back to the marginally-safer confines of the bowling-alley. Sure, they'd be pissed at him, but he didn't see them putting their lives on the line, making an effort to do something about the situation.

The phone wouldn't break, no matter how hard he squeezed.

Fuck, he thought. *I'm going through with it.*

He was eight steps closer to the bins when Tom's voice startled him. "You're doing great," the sonofabitch said. "Keep it up."

Mike ignored it; he was too scared to lift a finger, which was just about all he wanted to do at that moment.

He glanced down at the cell phone; the flashing antenna told him the phone was still out of service. He walked slowly – gingerly – towards the bins, and could smell the fetid, offensive contents. Bowling-alley pizza-boxes were stacked next to the large containers, slowly growing soggy in the rain.

Mike was surprised there were no scavenging rats in sight.

Too frightened to come out and play, he thought.

Another glance at the phone in his sweaty palm informed him, as it had before, that he might as well be carrying a pink dildo.

He turned and gave Tom an exaggerated shrug. Tom's shoulders slumped ever-so-slightly before he urged Mike to go a little farther.

Mike suddenly had the ability to give Tom the finger, and he made good use of it. Tom, surprisingly, didn't respond to it. Instead, he repeated the signal that meant he wanted Mike to keep going.

"Shit," Mike said, turning to face the containers. Something white suddenly emerged from beneath the largest one. A guttural noise escaped Mike's throat as he staggered backwards. Something must have tripped him, because the next thing he knew he was heading for the damp tarmac. The phone left his hand and clattered along the ground a few feet before shedding its cover and battery. Mike hit the ground with a *thump!* The bitter, coppery taste of blood told him that he'd bit his tongue upon impact, but he didn't care. All he cared about was the small, white thing approaching his feet. He crab-walked a few feet back in an attempt to escape it, but it was no use.

The Junior Mints box came to a halt against his foot at around the same time he realised what a fucking idiot he'd been.

In the doorway behind, Tom slapped a hand to his forehead in disbelief at what he had witnessed.

"Never gonna live *that* down," Mike whispered as he managed to climb to his feet. His ass was soaked, his mouth tasted like it was filled with pennies, and his pride – the little he still possessed – hurt like the Dickens. He brushed himself down and picked up the cell phone's pieces.

He reconnected the battery and slid the cover over until it clicked into place.

"It's okay," he whispered to Tom as the phone began to power up. "It's not broken."

Tom gave him two thumbs up.

"Fucking Junior Mints," he mumbled as he waited for the cell to do its thing. When it did, he almost wished it hadn't.

Beyoncé's 'Single Ladies' began to blare from the speaker as the Home menu loaded. He'd completely forgotten that it did that, and now he was in two minds whether to continue. The door Tom was standing in looked so inviting; five seconds, he could be back inside, pouring more shitty cocktails, telling Tom to go fuck himself.

If you liked it then you should have put a ring on it...

ADAM MILLARD

Mike saw something move to his right, and as he turned he couldn't believe he'd been so stupid.

Hundreds of them poured out of the wall as if it was giving birth to them. There were so many of them they were crawling over one another to reach him, and as he turned to run for Tom and the doorway, he felt them scale his back, his shoulders, crawling over him like the very fingers of death. He managed four steps before the impossible pain brought him to his knees. The beetles had him right where they wanted him. One of them peeled back his scalp as he flicked as many away as he could. His brain was suddenly exposed to the elements, and the rain peppering his grey-matter caused him to remember things from his childhood that he'd long since forgotten.

A birthday cake his grandmother made for him in the shape of R2D2.

His eyebrows were stripped away, along with an ear...

A terrible camping trip in which he'd fallen into an icy lake and almost drowned.

Lips, gone forever. Say bye-bye, lips. Two of the creatures began to fight over them. Mike watched, paralysed and wide-eyed as his eyelids were stripped away. He had no choice but to watch, now.

A broken mirror. A broken arm. Brush your

teeth, Mike. Brush them good. None of it made any sense; of course it didn't. His head was filling up with rainwater as the creatures feasted on his flesh.

At the end of the alley, Tom closed the door.

"So much for getting a signal," he said before explaining to Angelina what he'd just witnessed.

"Holy shit!" she gasped, throwing herself forward into Tom's arms. "I'm so sorry, Tom."

"Me too," Tom said. "They're gonna have to get Uwe Boll in to finish the movie. That really pisses me off."

There was a loud bang on the door which startled both Angelina and Tom. Tom stepped back and used Angelina as a shield.

"What the fuck are you doing?" Angelina screeched.

The door banged again. "Please!" a voice yelled. "Let me in!"

Tom let go of Angelina's shoulders and took another step back.

* * *

It's all looking a bit dire, Spike thought, what with the weather, the fact that his bar was trashed, and the millions of oversized beetles crawling around the city with nothing better to do than chew people up. The promising future was gone, replaced by a nightmare that he – and the rest of the city – would be lucky to survive.

He heard a groan to his right, and immediately snapped his head in that direction.

A man was on his knees, covered in the flesh-eating creatures. Spike knew there was nothing he could do, that the pool cue in his hand was more for display purposes than battle-engagement.

He would have run away had he not noticed the man standing in the doorway at the end of the street.

"Shit!" he said, watching as the door slowly closed. The man being skinned between Spike and the door said something about *camping* as the swarm made away with his right arm.

Spike knew he had to get to the door. It could be the door to more survivors, a safe-house, an airtight building where he would be safe until morning, or at least until the army showed up.

But there were so many bugs in the way. An entire sea of white, jester-faced beetles stood between him and the door. He doubted he'd be able to get past them, not without getting some on him.

There was only one thing for.

"Come on, Spikey-boy," he said, encouraging himself out loud as if it might prevent him from backing out of what he was about to do. He took a few steps back, looked at the sea of bugs, and glanced at the man on his knees whose head was dangling listlessly against his shoulder, the brains spilling slowly out of his skull. And then he began to run, the pool cue held out in front of him as if he was going to joust the living shit out of the beetles.

He didn't, of course. That would be ridiculous.

At the very last moment he brought the cue down. As it made contact with the ground, Spike felt himself being launched over the kneeling man's back. He was pole-vaulting over a dead guy, and he couldn't help the strange exhilaration he felt as he realised he was going to make it.

His feet touched down on the other side of the mumbling dead man, and he didn't stop running until he slammed into the door.

"What the fuck are you doing?" a woman's voice screamed from the inside. Spike didn't think she was talking to him. He brought a fist up and banged as hard as he could. Those things were already scrambling towards him; he could hear the annoying sound as they neared.

"Please!" Spike yelled. "Let me in!"

He waited, listening. He knew they were in there, at least two of them, a man and a woman. What were they going to do? Leave him out to die with the other guy?

As Spike turned to find the creatures almost upon him, he realised that: *Yes, they're going to leave me out here to die with the other guy...*

A whimper he wasn't proud of escaped his

throat as he pushed back against the door. This was how it was going to end. Spike had had dreams of dying on-stage, being electrocuted while mic-testing for Jagger and the boys. "This isn't how it's supposed to happen," he whined. "Not like this."

One beetle scampered up his leg and he kicked it away.

The next thing he knew he was falling backwards. On the way down he saw what he thought was a ghost, and as he rolled back he heard a loud bang as the ghost slammed the door shut.

Staggering to his feet, he realised he was inside, and it wasn't a ghost at all.

It was a Goth-chick.

This must be heaven, he thought, and then something really heavy clouted him round the back of the head. "I coulda been a contender," he mumbled as the wooziness washed over him.

Everything went very dark, very fast.

* * *

Kyle knew they were outnumbered. Skinners were everywhere: crawling up buildings, along the ground, over windows and doors, there were just too damn many of them to take care of. The LAFD, LAPD, US Army and all its reserves would have trouble containing them.

"We're not going to win this!" Sherman howled, lifting the hose and spraying a small swarm that had broken away from the rest of the Skinners. "They're going in after the people in the apartments!"

"I can fucking *see* that!" Kyle said, uncoiling his own hose from around Sherman's legs. "We can't just let them die in their beds!"

Around sixty Skinners started crawling towards the truck. Kyle spotted them and quickly aimed his hose at them. They shot backwards as the pressurized insecticide – partially diluted by the water already in the apparatus system – made contact. The truth of it was: they just didn't have enough Buzz-Kill. Mixing it with the water had lessened its intensity, but those fuckers were still dying, albeit at a steadier pace, and that was all that mattered.

"I feel like Peter Venkman!" Sherman said, blasting his way through another group of approaching Skinners. They slowly evaporated, sizzling on the ground like eggs on a skillet. He grinned. "Yeah, that's me. Who ya" gonna call?"

"A fucking psychiatrist after this," Kyle said. From out of nowhere, a bug landed on his shoulder. He grabbed it by the shell and tossed it across the street. The swatch of material it had ripped from his collar dangled from its underside as it bounced along the curb.

Kyle sprayed it, sending it – and a hundred just like it – down the street where they began to sizzle and melt from the chemical onslaught.

"We can't do this all night," Kyle said.

"You're right," Sherman said. "I've got to get up early for a meeting." If it was an attempted joke, Kyle didn't get it.

"Jump into the truck," Kyle said. "Go! I'll keep these fuckers off you."

Sherman did as he was told. "Come on!" Sherman called as he made it safely in through the passenger-side door. "We need to regroup!"

There are two of us, Kyle thought. Hardly a group; barely even a duo…

He blasted the creatures nearest to him as far along the street as he could, buying him just enough time to make it to the truck. He turned and raced for the door, which Sherman, he assumed – he *hoped* – would open at the last minute. Thankfully, he wasn't as stupid as he looked and waited for Kyle to get close enough before pulling the lever and swinging the door out.

"Any other bright ideas?" Kyle asked, swinging his legs into position. He slammed the door behind him. The Skinners slammed against the door, such was their eagerness to feed. Kyle turned the key in the ignition. The truck roared into life.

"We need to get moving," Kyle said. His finger pointed towards the rear-view mirror. Kyle didn't need to turn his head to know what the geek was pointing at. He could hear them; he could feel the truck slowly rocking from side-to-side as more Skinners clambered aboard.

"We're almost out of fuel," Kyle reminded Sherman. "We'll be lucky to make it out of this street."

"Then make it out of this street!" Sherman said, his eyes filled with panic.

Kyle slammed his foot down on the accelerator.

*   *   *

"There was no need to knock him out," Angelina said.

Tom, still holding the pool cue that the guy had dropped during his dramatic entrance, had to disagree. "He could be anyone," he said. "Besides, you almost killed me back in the toilets because you thought I was a rapist. What makes you think this guy's not just in this apocalypse for the repopulation?"

"Don't be stupid."

"Hey, didn't you ever see *28 Days Later*?" Tom said. "The hint's in the title as to how long it was before the army started collecting women."

The man on the floor began to stir; blood had matted his hair together at the back of his head. Tom didn't trust men who had more hair than he did; this guy had enough to choke a donkey.

Angelina dropped to her haunches and began to help the newcomer to his feet.

"What the hell are you doing?" Tom asked, swinging the pool cue like a Jedi. "Don't be surprised if he goes for you—"

"*Goes* for me, Tom? This isn't a zombie outbreak." She gently helped the man to his feet; Tom didn't know why, but he felt more than a little jealous of the tenderness Angelina was showing the guy.

"I'm okay," the man said, rubbing the back of his head. There was already an egg there, and it hurt like a sonofabitch. "I was just trying to get away from those…those *things*." He turned, saw Tom wielding the pool cue – *his* pool cue – and said, "I take it you knew the guy getting turned inside out out there?"

Tom was surprised this newcomer didn't recognize him. He thought about introducing himself, but decided against it when he realised that it didn't matter anymore, that the playing-field had been levelled, once again, when those things crawled up from the bowels of hell to wreak havoc on the unassuming populace. If this shit-storm was widespread, people who used to *be* somebody had been relegated to peasants, like the rest of the country.

Why did it have to hit LA? We're all important, here…

"He was a friend of mine," Tom lied. "We were filming a movie when it happened." *Fuck it.* "I'm Tom Harker. You might recognize me from *Lethal Agent*."

The man frowned.

"*Lethal Agent 2*?" Tom said.

"I don't—"

"What's the matter with people these days?" Tom snapped. "Does nobody give a shit about good old-fashioned action movies anymore? I remember when you couldn't walk down the street without someone mentioning Stallone." He scratched his head. "*Lethal Agent 3*? No? Terence Stamp played the baddie?" When the man shrugged, and Angelina sniggered, Tom decided to quit while he was behind. "Fuck it." He turned and made his way over to the bar.

"I'm Spike," the man said, offering his hand. Angelina shook it, and was unsurprised to find he was still a little shaky. "What's wrong with your friend?"

Angelina snorted. "He's an asshole. Don't worry about him."

"I wasn't going to," he said. "How many more

of you are there?"

Angelina's expression faltered. "Oh, no, it's just me and the asshole, Spike. Did you see anyone else out there?"

"It's a ghost-town," he said. It was the truth. Apart from the cat, and the poor bastard muttering about camping, he hadn't seen another soul. "How many of those things *are* there? I mean, there has to be more of us."

"I'm thinking a lot of people won't be waking up in the morning," she said. "The quake hit quite late; those things came just after. I'm guessing a lot of people are tucked up in bed."

"Best place for them," Spike said. "My bar was overrun with those fucking demons. Killed most of my regulars."

Angelina brightened, which was perhaps not the reaction he was expecting. She had, Spike thought, a wonderful smile. "Which bar?"

"Hard Rock Café," Spike said.

"Oh, I think you barred me last year." Her smile disappeared.

"No way," he said. "I only bar ugly people."

Smooth, he thought. *Smooth and completely fucking ridiculous.* Now was not the time for stupid pick-up lines. In fact, pick-up lines were *never* good; the current situation just added to the wrongness.

"We should…" Angelina began to say, and then cocked her head to the side as if listening. "Do you hear that?"

Spike did. It was a siren, dopplering through the night.

"Well it's about damn time," Tom said, pouring himself a large shot of whiskey.

The siren neared, high-pitched and interrupted occasionally by a deeper, more erratic tone. It wasn't a siren the police employed, and Tom didn't think it was an ambulance.

"Maybe we should go out?" Angelina opined. "They won't know we're in here. If it's here to help—"

Just then, there was an almighty crash. Wall exploded inward; the Elvis Presley pinball machine flew through the air, almost hitting Spike. Angelina grabbed his arm and yanked him to the ground as debris continued to fly across the room. Pictures of famous people flew down the alleys. An image of James Dean rapidly skidded down Alley 9, where it took out all ten pins. Dust and miniscule debris filled the air as everything started to settle.

Over by the bar, Tom began to cough. He was delighted when he saw the glass in his hand still contained the golden liquid he'd poured only a few seconds earlier. He was not so happy, however, when the newly-arrived fire-truck that now took up the majority of the foyer made one final *honk!* Tom dropped the glass and it shattered into a hundred pieces, spilling much-needed whiskey everywhere.

The door to the truck flew open. One man, wearing firefighter fatigues, spilled from within, coughing and spluttering as if he'd just left Snoop Dogg's apartment. He dropped to his knees and began to spit. Just then, a second man climbed from the truck. He looked a little odd – in the Richard Simmons sense of the word – with his purple tie thrown across his shoulder like Biggles. As he sucked in air, Angelina noticed the gap in his teeth, the one large enough to park a Humvee in.

"*That* told them," he said to the spluttering firefighter. "Maybe you should have slowed down at that last turning."

The guy on the floor coughed. "We had to lose them, didn't we?" he said. He pushed himself up from the ground and began to survey their surroundings. "Hello?" he called; it was impossible to see through the dancing dust, but Kyle was pretty sure he'd seen the shocked and contorted face of a woman as they'd crashed through the wall.

"Ahem," Tom said, casually picking plaster out of a clean, unbroken glass. "You can't park there."

Kyle stepped over a pile of bricks. There were dead bodies beneath the fallen wall. At first, Kyle panicked. He thought he was responsible for the bodies, but then he saw the lack of skin and the glistening crimson limbs beneath the bricks. These people had been skinned; hitting them with a fire-truck hadn't made much difference to their predicament.

"I'd say we need to block the hole you've left," Tom said, sipping furtively from his dusty glass, "but I really don't care anymore."

The man in the brown suit appraised the rear of the truck, before turning and offering two thumbs up. "It's wedged in the wall," he said, a little too excited for Tom's liking. "We should be okay."

"Where the fuck did *you* come from?" Angelina said, dusting herself down. "You nearly killed Stripe, here—"

"Spike," the long-haired man corrected, though she continued regardless.

"And you've put a huge hole in the side of our sanctuary. I'm guessing you weren't sent to save us."

The firefighter shook his head. "We're just trying to save ourselves long enough to make a difference," he said. "Those…things ate my buddies. The whole block's crawling with them."

"I don't suppose you know what they are?" Tom said. "Or where they came from?"

"Sherman's your man for information," the firefighter, Kyle, said as he exploded, once again, in a coughing fit.

Sherman – he of the brown, suede suit and

purple tie debacle – explained everything to the enraptured trio. How he'd fought the Skinners back in '93 with machine-guns. Okay, so he embellished the truth a little. He didn't think they would take him seriously if he told them his last encounter with the creatures had been pretty much taken care of by a geriatric lady and a can of extra-hold Perm-A-Lot.

"So how do we *kill* them?" Spike asked when Sherman finished sprouting nonsense. "Other than picking them off with Uzis?"

"Well, the truck's loaded with insecticide," Kyle said, "but we don't have nearly enough to take out all of them." He remembered the reason why the truck had ploughed into Lucky Strike Lanes in the first place. "Oh, yeah, and we have no fuel, so unless one of you owns a pretty large tow-truck, that thing's a permanent fixture."

"Great," Tom said. He raised his glass, as if in toast. "To the end of the world," he said before knocking back the whiskey as if it was going out of fashion.

Something exploded a few streets away; the blast was quickly followed by screams and shouts of confusion.

"So we just sit tight and wait for those things to find a way in here and pick us apart," Tom said. He was searching around in the rubble for something, which he found and lifted for all to see: the whiskey bottle. "And I'm going to get very, very drunk in the meantime. I reckon having the skin ripped from me like a Thanksgiving turkey will hurt a lot less if I'm tipsy."

"That's not all we have to worry about," Sherman said. His muted announcement suggested he was ashamed of himself for keeping what he was about to share to himself, at least from Kyle, who he'd had more than enough chances to tell.

"What do you mean?" Kyle said. "Sherman, for fuck's sake, what else do you know?"

Sherman grit his teeth; the gap was so pronounced that Kyle reckoned he could squeeze his big, firefighter fist in there, and would if the prick didn't tell them what the hell was going on.

"When I said I worked at the lab," he said, "I wasn't lying." He paused, took a deep breath, then said, "Those cars down in the lot didn't belong to people who had died while in the company's employ."

"I *knew* that was bullshit," Kyle said, before urging the geek to continue.

"They belong to volunteers, people with nothing left to live for, people who don't mind being genetically modified, or cryogenically frozen for a couple of years."

"And you're trying to tell us what, exactly?" Angelina said, feeling ill all of a sudden. Her ashen complexion had very little to do with her Goth make-up – which had mostly rubbed off – but was down to the fact that she'd never been so terrified in her entire life.

"That we've known about Skinners long enough to give us valuable information," Sherman said. He'd lost his previous enthusiasm, and was now speaking as if someone had a gun to his head. "BioTex wanted us to make something capable of taking *them* on, should they ever surface again."

"Holy shit!" Spike said. "What could you possibly create that's worse than those evil fucking clown-bugs?"

"Superhuman Skinnermen," Sherman said, as if it was the most normal sentence he'd ever constructed. "All of their strengths, none of their weaknesses. Their skin has been treated with Buzz-Kill. If one of those things even *licks* a Skinnerman, it'll shrivel up and die quicker than Charlie Sheen's liver at an all-you-can-drink buffet."

Tom laughed before upturning the bottle and emptying the contents into his throat.

"This just keeps getting better and better," Angelina said. "And when should we expect these horrible fucking aberrations to make an appearance?"

Sherman glanced down at his watch. "Well, that's the thing," he said. "I would have thought they'd…

*　　*　　*

The clown-faced men stood upright in their opaque cubicles. Their teeth chittered and chattered, layer upon layer of razor-sharp pins moving from side-to-side as they slept. Machinery whined and whirred all around them. Tubes entered orifices, providing them with food, sustenance, enough to keep them alive while they awaited the Skinners' return. Whether they dreamed or not remained unknown. *Do Skinnermen dream of electric sheep?* Of course not. Why would they?

They twitched in their temporary prisons, almost as if they could sense what was happening out in the city. They needed to be freed; they relied on some fucker with a lanyard to press the button on the console at the front of the room, the one that would release them, the one that would save the world from the most brutal Skinner attack there had ever been.

Nobody was there to press the button, though.

There were only the bugs, scrambling across the tiles – stopping momentarily to glance up, and possibly admire, the standing, hominid version of themselves. The swarm didn't know that these things, these monstrosities, were their adversaries. They were blissfully unaware, as they swamped over everything in sight, that should one of them accidentally press the "Open" button, their entire species would go the way of the dinosaurs.

They were blissfully unaware right up until one of the Skinners chewed through something it shouldn't have.

The whole lab exploded, along with the curious swarm and mankind's only hope.

*   *   *

"...**h**ave been released by now," Sherman finished. The explosion rocked the city; Sherman knew exactly what had happened. "Well, I guess that's it, then. Let's all just get drunk and…" he glanced around at the debris, "...well, I was going to say have a few games of bowling, but unless one of you know where there's a brush, I guess we're fucked."

"That's not the attitude I expect from a clever guy like you," Kyle said. If they had any chance of surviving this, they had to work together. Sherman was the brains, and he was obsolete once he started drinking. Kyle couldn't let it happen.

"Look, we tried," Sherman said. "The Skinnermen have exploded, nobody's coming to rescue us, and there's a good chance I've just shit myself." He paused and gave his pants an embarrassed tug. He'd completely forgotten there was a woman present, not that it would have made the slightest difference.

"Toilets are that way," Angelina told him.

"Thanks." He turned and did a strange little run past the fire truck all the way to the door.

"He's...*odd*," Angelina said.

Kyle nodded. "He might just be the only chance we've got of making it through this."

"Let's fucking hope not," Tom said, swigging long and hard from a bottle of Amaretto Sour. "Guy's just shit his pants."

*　　*　　*

"**P**athetic. *Really*, Sherman?" he said as he got cleaned up. "You couldn't hold it in? You couldn't control yourself?"

He had never considered death before. Sure, he'd pondered what might follow, whether there was an afterlife or if it was just like before being born – not that he could recall how *that* felt.

He'd never had to consider actual death, or that it might be just around the corner. At the start of the day everything had been normal; he'd gone to work, as always, on his bicycle. On his lunch-break he'd eaten two corners of a salad sandwich and an apple; the afternoon had flown by due to how busy he'd kept himself priming twelve cockroaches for dissection. It had been a very normal day, as far as they went.

Now look at me, he thought. *Shitty pants round my ankles waiting for Skinners to bite me a new asshole.*

He cleaned himself as best as he could. It was difficult with the limited amount of toilet paper he had to work with. As he washed his hands after – why he bothered, even he didn't know – he stared off into the corner of the room. It was then that he saw something dangling from a rusted pipe on the wall.

"I'll be damned," he said.

* * *

Kyle held the fly-tape by its string. He was a little dubious about holding anything Sherman had to offer after what he'd just done, but he had to admit that it wasn't a terrible idea.

"Could it work?" Angelina asked. "I mean, if we could find something sticky enough, would they go for it?"

Sherman nodded. "They would if we put bait next to it."

"And what? They just crawl on it and get

stuck?" Tom had begun to slur his words from the amount of alcohol he'd consumed. "Sounds like a bit of a long-shot."

"It's a lot of a long-shot," Kyle said, trying to maintain his composure, "but it's better than anything you've suggested."

Tom gave him the finger.

"Where are we going to get something sticky?" Spike asked. It was a good question, and one that he seemed proud of. "This is hardly a glue factory."

Despite the small setback, Sherman remained upbeat. "You're forgetting what I do for a living."

"You create *monsters*," Tom spat from the bar. "Little fuckers with a taste for human flesh."

"Pipe down, Tom," Angelina said. "You're starting to sound like a little bitch."

Tom gave her the finger. It seemed to be his answer for everything.

Sherman continued. "If I could get my hands on some resin, or perhaps even beeswax—"

"I work at Hollywood Wax," Angelina suddenly blurted. "Is that the right kind of stuff?"

Kyle didn't let Sherman answer. "It's too far away," he said. "It would be suicide." Angelina looked duly deflated, and exhaled with disappointment.

"What about chemicals?" Kyle said. "There's got to be a cleaning-room somewhere in the building; those shoes don't wash themselves."

"You're right," Sherman said. "If we can find some old sheets, and something to make the compound from, I think we've got a shot."

Another explosion rocked the night, but for the first time since those things crawled up from out of their godforsaken hellholes, the survivors had a clear agenda. Over by the bar, Tom hissed. He would give it another half-hour before executing a plan of his own.

*   *   *

The beetles crawled over the mangled wrecks of cars, pouring in through the shattered windows to get to the goodies inside. As people tried to flee the city, they'd underestimated the amount of traffic there would be on the freeway. The cars and trucks that hadn't collided were trapped, wedged between the wrecks of those that had. People tried to run for it, but were soon swallowed up by the insatiable Skinner swarms. Men and women were stripped where they fell. The bloody, screaming leftovers tried to drag themselves to safety, only to discover that life without skin would be short and brutal.

A family – nuclear, with two dogs in the backseat – decided there was nothing else for it; there was no way they were allowing those hellish creatures free reign over their bodies. The father said a prayer, loaded the shotgun, and proceeded to pick off the people who he loved more than anything in the world. The car shook with each blast; the dogs barked, and then whimpered as he did to them what he had to do to himself. He turned the gun over, and was about to pull the trigger when he glanced down and saw that his finger, the one he'd intended to use to end his life, was gone. One of the white beetles was in the car, sitting on his chest. His finger moved back and forth in the creature's mouth as it gnawed it to the knuckle.

"Fuck," the father mumbled, as more of them filtered in through the bottom of the car. He was to suffer along with the other poor bastards on the freeway. *At least*, he thought as the pain ripped through him and the bugs crawled over him entirely, *I spared my family*.

The Skinners fed well. A choir of car-horns filled the night as a result of skeletal faces slumped dead against their respective steering-wheels.

The creatures moved on, leaving behind the smoking, stinking trail of cars and the lifeless, bleeding corpses contained within.

*   *   *

It wasn't much of a cleaning room; it was more a

cupboard under the stairs. As Kyle began to hand things back to Sherman, who was dancing with anticipation behind them, he reeled off what he could see and what he could reach, ignoring the things he knew would be useless. As creative as he believed Sherman to be, he didn't think the guy would be able to make glue from a half-empty cherry shoe-polish and a box of luminous drinking-straws.

"Wouldn't it be great if there was glue in there?" Sherman said, hopping from one foot to the other. Angelina shot him a glance that asked the question: *seriously?* "Yeah, you're right," he added. "Stupid idea."

Kyle pulled something out that looked like a statue. Blowing the dust from it, he said, "Cthulhu." He handed it to Sherman, who gave it a cursory glance before handing the grotesque figure to Spike.

"Rhymes with glue, I guess," Spike said, wiping dust from the thing's tentacle-face. "Don't suppose you've been working on raising this fella from the ocean, have you?"

Sherman shook his head. "We tried once," he said. "Turns out that none of the Old Ones like to take orders from humans."

"I should feel comforted that you know all this stuff about ancient gods and prehistoric clown-bugs," she said, "but I'm finding it difficult not to scream right now."

On his knees, Kyle handed Sherman another sheet. This one was blue, patterned with several cartoon characters that none of them recognised. "Is that enough yet?"

"Sheets, yes," Sherman said. "Now, there wouldn't happen to be a vat of tanglefoot in there, would there?"

Kyle returned to the cupboard. He had no idea what tanglefoot was, but he guessed it would be the perfect tool for the job, which meant there would be none, which saved him from bothering to look for it altogether. There were eight tubs near the back, hermetically sealed and stacked. Kyle dragged the containers into the light where he could see the label.

"Fucking *starch*," he said, dismissing it as useless. He moved as if to push the tubs back when Sherman's indubitable whine stopped him.

"Wait!" he said. "Did you just say starch?"

Kyle turned. "Yeah. Why? Can we stiffen them to death?"

Sherman began to mumble as he struggled to explain what he could do with starch without getting excited.

"Whoa, one sentence at a time," Kyle said. "Do you want the starch out, or not?"

"Give me the starch," Sherman said, as coolly as he could.

They took the materials out to the hall. Spike and Angelina laid out the sheets while Sherman mixed the powdered starch with warm water. Over at the bar, Tom cracked open a bottle of champagne and tried to remember the name of the guy, his friend the director, who'd died out front an hour or so ago. "I want to say Matthew," he sniggered to himself. Turning his attention to the furore in the middle of the room, he said, "Look at you all. Too *stupid* to know when to just…lie down and die." He was barely comprehensible, which was just as well since Kyle was looking for a reason to knock him out.

"Is this going to work?" Spike asked, handing Angelina the scrunched corner of the sheet they were unfolding.

"Either that or we're just going to end up with some nice, crisp sheets," she said.

Sherman began to spread the thick, gloopy paste over the flattened sheets. He hummed jovially as he worked, which was slightly annoying, considering the circumstances. Kyle thought it was a good time to broach the subject of transport.

"The truck's no good," he said. "You don't need me to tell you that."

Sherman continued to smear the sheets with liquid starch. It looked like pigeon-shit without the brown bits. "I was hoping somebody would volunteer to fetch us a car," he said, then continued to whistle as if his suggestion had been something small and banal.

"What, go *outside*?" Spike asked. "Out there, where those *things* are?"

"Hmmmm, I can see why that might be a problem," Sherman said, scratching his chin with white, sticky fingers. "It's either that or we just stick to the original plan. Sit here, wait for them to find us, then try to convince them not to eat us."

Sarcasm, it seemed, was not as easy to kill as people.

"I'll go," Kyle said. Just like that.

"No," Spike said. "I've got experience hotwiring cars. I can get us a vehicle."

Kyle wasn't about to argue. Truthfully, he was scared shitless; the whole thing made no sense, and that terrified him. "I saw a Focus across the street," he said.

"When you were barrelling towards us at fifty-mile-an-hour?" Tom slurred.

Kyle snarled. "Why don't you just shut the fuck up? Huh? Before I punch you so hard you'll have to take off your shoes to shit."

Tom didn't know what that meant, but assuming it was a direct threat, he turned his back and continued to drown his sorrows alone.

"I'll get the Focus round to the back," Spike said. "You just have the sheets ready."

"Pop the trunk as soon as you pull up," Sherman said. "We'll hook the sheets on. I'm forty percent sure that this could work."

"Forty?" Angelina gasped. "Wow, that much, huh?"

"At least thirty," Sherman corrected. "Give or take."

"Let's get this show on the road," Kyle said. "While we still have a city to save."

Spike made his way to the back door, paused for a moment as if to reflect on what a miserable existence it had been, then said, "I'll be back," in broken Austrian. As he raced off into the night, the other survivors merely shrugged it off as unintelligible nonsense caused by fear.

Not how he'd wanted them to interpret what might be his final words.

*   *   *

The Focus was where Kyle said it would be. The only problem was that it was teeming with Skinners. In fact, there wasn't a surface out there that didn't have at least one beetle scurrying along it. The noise they made – *gah*! It was enough to drive a man crazy – reminded Spike of a band he was forced to play back at the bar. Some alternative, pussy-punk quintet that made you wish you had the balls to do what Van Gogh did, and lop the fuckers off.

Was it too late to turn back? The opportunity of doing anything remotely heroic, which was what he'd intended when he'd optioned himself, seemed to have disappeared. The Skinners were everywhere; thousands – nay – *millions* of them. Scurrying and clambering, skittering and scrambling, he was just about to run out of synonyms when something clicked against his boot-heel, sending him hurtling toward the Focus with complete disregard for his own safety.

If they're going to get me, they've got their work cut out.

* * *

At the back door, Kyle, Angelina and Sherman anxiously waited. They could hear distant sirens; people still trying to escape the madness, somehow. Rain continued to fleck the tarmac, and there was a shallow stream running along the curb as the downpour continued.

"It's a pity they're not allergic to rainwater," Sherman said.

"I bet that's not the first time you've held sticky sheets, geek-boy, is it?" Tom drunkenly asked from the hallway. He sniggered. "Yeah, now you know how your momma feels."

"I never noticed before," Angelina said as she turned to face Tom, "but you're a real asshole."

Tom, not perturbed in the slightest by her sudden attack, smiled crookedly. "Well, nobody asked your opinion, sweetheart. Little Miss B-movie…Princess-fucking-Vampira…I—"

Unfortunately for him, he didn't have the opportunity to finish that sentence. The Focus came hurtling in reverse down the side-street, swerving erratically, knocking over trashcans, before finally rolling over the still-slumped corpse of Mike Starkweather, who folded beneath the wheels as if he was Sherman's Buffy cut-out.

Kyle pulled Angelina away from the door just in time, as the Focus continued to careen out of control. As it burst through the door – taking the wall on either side with it – hundreds of Skinners flew into the hallway.

"What the—" Tom mumbled in the second he had before the creatures scampered over him. He began to flail around like a madman, knocking only a few off.

"Quick!" Kyle said, pulling Angelina to her feet. The creatures were too interested in the lunatic making a song and dance behind them to notice there were others present.

Sherman was wedged beneath the vehicle, though its wheels hadn't gone over him. He was thankful for that, though not for the sliver of wooden door that had embedded itself in his right arm. He pulled the splinter out, hissing as the pain tore through his very existence. Suddenly arms hooked him beneath his own, and he was pulled backward, dazed and more than a little pissed off with Spike for driving like a maniac.

"Y'okay?" Kyle asked once Sherman was clear of the car.

"Sure," he said. "I get run over, like, *all* the time…"

The sound of chattering creatures ended the conversation.

More Skinners crawled up Tom's legs, and before long he fell silent. Teeth clicked and whirred, chewing him up, stripping him of a body that he'd been perfecting since childhood. Thin strips of flesh landed on the ground next to where he stood, only to be snatched up and carried away by Skinners who were in no mood to share.

Kyle pulled open the driver's side door; Spike was alive, barely. His legs, right the way up to where his cock should have been, were nothing but bone and sinew.

No wonder he couldn't drive in a straight line. His feet were nowhere near the pedals.

In fact, his feet were still outside in the rain

being picked at by four ravenous beetles.

"Get in the car!" Kyle said. Angelina didn't need telling twice, which was unusual for a Goth girl of her age. Sherman was already lying on the back seat, strewn out like drying laundry.

Kyle rushed around to the rear of the Focus. Every Skinner that had clung to the car for dear life as Spike had steered it, in a fashion, toward the bowling alley was now crawling over Tom's fallen body. The guy was an asshole, but even *he* didn't deserve to go out like that.

Picking up one of the sticky sheets, Kyle threw it over the feeding beetles. There were high-pitched utterances from the swarm as they suddenly found themselves unable to move. The sheet clung to their shells, preventing them from escaping it.

Kyle tried the trunk. *Shit, I thought I said…*

There was an audible *clunk!* and the trunk opened half an inch. Kyle glanced up to see Angelina's raised thumb through the rear window.

Quickly, he affixed one sheet to the inside of the trunk and tossed the others into the back. Spreading the sheet haphazardly, he made his way to the front of the car.

Spike was dead; Kyle wasn't a doctor, but there was no coming back from having your legs, cock and balls gnawed off. His head slumped listlessly against the headrest; his tongue dangled just as lifelessly from his lips.

He pulled Spike out. Angelina was about to complain that Kyle was being a little overzealous until she realised that the rocker had been shuffled loose of his mortal coil. "Oh, is he…"

"Yup," Kyle said. He climbed into the car and slammed the door shut. "Make sure your windows are closed. We don't want any nasty surprises once we get out there."

He pushed the stick into gear and pulled forward, leaving Lucky Strike Lanes needing more than just its customary bi-decadal makeover. Tom was dead, Spike was dead, Joe, Luke and Freddy were dead…

Bump.

Oh, and the guy in the middle of the street, slumped over like rashers of undercooked bacon – he was definitely dead.

*   *   *

Sherman felt responsible, somehow. The creatures hadn't been created – unlike the Skinnermen, which he'd played no small part in – and yet he'd known about them, kept them a secret all this time.

And now look: They were free of the earth and tearing the place apart. If that didn't at least make him partially culpable, he didn't know what did.

It was the reason why he now hung out the trunk of the Focus, grasping the adhesive sheet, catching as many of the fucking things as he could with the sticky trap. He'd never dreamt he would have to atone for decades of silence by putting himself at risk like this, but it was the least he could do.

The *very* least.

"Keep going to the end of this block!" he yelled back. "This sheet's nearly full. I'm gonna have to do a switchover at the next turning."

He couldn't believe it was working. The Skinners were coming from everywhere. Alleyways and side-streets that they would have overlooked otherwise spewed forth a torrent of clown-faced beetles, and the first thing they went for was the guy hanging out the back of the moving car. What they hadn't counted on, though, was the sticky net that was trailing behind, and as they scurried onto it, they became instantly stuck, glued for disposal later.

They kept on coming. Kyle and Angelina were just as bewildered as the tour of the city continued and dawn reared its ugly head over the horizon. With the cessation of the rain came more Skinners, as if they were suddenly encouraged by the drying tarmac beneath their spindly legs.

"Come get some," Sherman said as the

creatures continued to adhere to the material. He released the full sheet and made a mental note of where it finished up. It was no use collecting the Skinners and not knowing where they were later on. Besides, he was pretty sure that the stickiness would only last for a while; they weren't stupid creatures, at least not compared to say, turkeys, or Snooki. They would figure out a way of breaking free of their bonds eventually. Time was of the essence.

Sherman was preparing the next sheet when something caused him to stop.

The ground was shaking. At first it was just a low thrum, but quickly escalated to a much more powerful tremor.

Kyle must have felt it, too, as the car began to swerve left and right as he fought to keep it under control.

"Another fucking quake?" Angelina asked, finally realising she hadn't been wearing her seatbelt. As she buckled up, she saw the huge crack tearing the road apart in front of them. "Kyle, look out!"

It was too late. Kyle slammed the brakes on, but forward momentum and the slick road carried them into the widening aperture. Sherman, realising what was about to happen, muttered something quietly before pulling the trunk shut.

The darkness was a welcome alternative to what he might have seen on the way into the hole.

The sound of metal twisting and Skinners screeching as the car descended into the opening reminded Sherman of something someone once said: *Darkness cannot drive out darkness. Only light can do that.*

"Martin Luther King," he whispered to nobody in particular as something skittered over the car while it continued to plummet. The unmistakeable chirrup of clown-faced beetles came from all sides. "No, wait, it might have been Stephen Ki—"

*   *   *

Darkness. The stench of death. The occasional rattle as a Skinner scrambled over the car's crumpled shell. Sherman was certain the others were dead. He hadn't heard a sound from them since awakening almost half an hour ago. If they were alive, surely they would have started a conversation about something, no matter how insipid. Sherman didn't expect to hear them playing I-Spy, but he expected to hear…something.

Finally, he heard something, but it didn't come from the front of the car. It came from above, so far up that Sherman finally realised just how far they had fallen into the fissure.

This must be how Jessica McClure felt, he

thought.

The noise came again; a fizzing sound, almost electric. Sherman had no idea what it was, but he knew it wasn't the Skinners. They were reacting to it with panic, sheer consternation. He could hear them chittering, and each time the noise came they squealed, a porcine *squee* that suggested they weren't having a very good time up there.

Sherman began to laugh.

Something was happening to the Skinners, something terrible. Sherman could hear the rotors of passing helicopters. The cavalry had arrived, and from the noise the Skinners were making, they had more than a Ford Focus and a batch of sticky sheets at their disposal.

Almost an hour passed. Sherman didn't mind; he was in perhaps the safest place in LA. Unless, of course, there was another quake, one that undid the aperture and squished the car and its contents like a juice-box. He tried not to think about it.

He was still not thinking about it when there was a thud on the roof of the car, then the sound of metal-on-metal.

"Got it!" a voice said, as the car began to squeak from movement. It was, Sherman thought, what a Transformer having a shit might sound like.

A few seconds later, the car was swinging left and right. Sherman adjusted his position in the trunk, knowing he was being rescued. He didn't want to emerge looking like a Chilean miner, and so straightened his purple tie. More voices hollered at one another as the car was hoisted from the crack; Sherman could hear Skinners being annihilated in the background. It was music to his ears. He wondered whether they'd located the sheets he'd dropped along the street. If not, he would show them, and they would thank him. He'd probably get a medal.

The car's tires hissed as it was placed on the tarmac. A gruff voice instructed somebody to open the trunk; another voice reported the two dead people in the front of the car. Poor bastards had been skinned as the cracked windows had done nothing to shield them from the creatures.

Sherman didn't know whether to laugh or cry as the trunk cautiously opened. Guns were trained on him, and so he came out with his arms raised.

Thinking of his earlier misdemeanour, he couldn't help thinking that *now* would be a good time to shit his pants.

"Don't shoot!" he said. "I'm unarmed and…I work for the *government*! I know the Skinners!"

A man stepped up. Burly, bald, looking like he could bench-press the car if he really wanted to, he wore army fatigues. A cigar was wedged into the side of his mouth. "You know about the *Skinners*, huh?" he grunted.

Sherman nodded frantically. "I know *everything*!" he said. "I can hel—"

The bald gorilla lifted his gun and fired two shots into Sherman's face. Sherman fell back into the trunk of the Focus. The gruff Major walked casually toward the car and slammed the trunk.

"Clean it up," he instructed the soldiers surrounding the vehicle. "Clean it all up."

*   *   *

"*And finally, the clean-up continues following the devastating series of earthquakes which killed almost half a million Los Angeles residents last week, including the actress and model Kim Kardashian, the artist formerly known as Justin Bieber, and all of the X-Factor Live tour's acts, as well as 458,000 actual people. The quake will go down in the history books as the most deadly since the Shaanxi earthquake of 1556. Despite only measuring 6.2 on the Richter-Sca—*"

Lydia twisted the radio-knob until she got the desired effect. She was sick of hearing about the damn earthquake in LA. The media was loving it, of course. This was their bread-and-butter, a story worth dragging their limey asses out of bed for. It would continue to annoy the living shit out of her until some Philippine typhoon took over, or until a tsunami washed over the coast of New Zealand, filling at least three swimming-pools and washing away Ned McGraw's Ute.

Lydia spotted a man walking along the side of the freeway, his thumb extended. She couldn't see his face; the coat he wore had a hood, and it was pulled up due to the continual rain.

"If it's not one thing," Lydia said, steering the car over to the side of the road, "it's another."

She wasn't one for picking up hitchhikers, but she had a long journey ahead. It might be good to have some company.

Beats listening to the radio…

She stopped the car a few feet in front of the guy so that he knew he had a ride, so long as he was going in the right direction and didn't look like an absolute psychopath.

He walked around to the passenger side and opened the door. As he climbed in, Lydia tried to get a look at his face, but the hood was doing a really good job of shielding it. There was a strange burnt smell, as if the guy had recently been to a bonfire, or perhaps *in* one.

"You can take that down in here," she laughed. "I promise I'll keep the sun-roof closed."

The guy didn't laugh. He did, however, make a strange chirruping sound. Lydia suddenly felt very uncomfortable, and was in two minds whether to ask the guy to get out.

Then he turned to face her, and she saw that he looked nothing like a psychopath.

He looked like a clown; his white, powdery face flaked here and there, his red nose looked striking against its pallid surroundings.

"Oh, my God!" Lydia screamed as the clown opened its mouth, and a thousand pin-teeth began to whir. The screaming didn't last for long, though.

It never does, thought the Skinnerman as he began to feed. *It never does…*

ABOUT THE AUTHOR

Adam Millard is the author of thirteen novels and more than a hundred short stories. Best known for his post-apocalyptic fiction, Adam also writes fantasy-horror books for children. He lives in Wolverhampton, England, with his wife, Zoe, and their son, Phoenix.